MW00510694

BETTER A DINNER OF HERBS

Better is a dinner of herbs where love is
than a stalled ox and hatred therewith.
—*Proverbs 15.17*

BETTER
A DINNER
OF HERBS

A Novel by
Byron Herbert Reece

Foreword by Hugh Ruppersburg

Brown Thrasher Books
THE UNIVERSITY OF GEORGIA PRESS
Athens and London

This book is dedicated to the memory of
Bill (William Wiseman) Lance,
who taught me something of courage.

Published in 1992 as a Brown Thrasher Book
by the University of Georgia Press, Athens, Georgia 30602
Foreword © 1992 by the University of Georgia Press
All rights reserved

The paper in this book meets the guidelines for
permanence and durability of the Committee on
Production Guidelines for Book Longevity of the
Council on Library Resources.

Printed in the United States of America

96 95 94 93 92   P   5 4 3 2 1

Library of Congress Cataloging in Publication Data

Reece, Byron Herbert, 1917–1958.
    Better a dinner of herbs : a novel / by Byron Herbert Reece ;
foreword by Hugh Ruppersburg.
        p.   cm.
    "Brown thrasher books."
    ISBN 0-8203-1489-7 (pbk. : alk. paper)
    I. Ruppersburg, Hugh M.   II. Title.
[PS3535.E245B4   1992]
813'.54—dc20   92-22952
                                                          CIP

British Library Cataloging in Publication Data available

Better a Dinner of Herbs was originally published in 1950
by E. P. Dutton & Co., New York, New York.

CONTENTS

FOREWORD

Hugh Ruppersburg

Byron Herbert Reece's *Better a Dinner of Herbs* was published by E. P. Dutton in 1950 to generally favorable reviews. Reece had labored on the novel since 1945, often at night, since during the day he worked his parents' farm near Blood Mountain in North Georgia. He had published in 1945 a volume of poems, *Ballad of the Bones*. Later in 1950 he published a second collection, *Bow Down in Jericho*. Both received admiring notice, and they were followed in the next eight years by several more volumes. But a poet's fame is fleeting. Reece was not a publicity seeker, and he passed most of his life in a relatively isolated part of the literary world. Though after his suicide in 1958 he was much mourned by those who knew him, today his name is virtually unknown outside his native state.

This is a pity. Reece was a poet of striking freshness and originality. He favored the dignified simplicity of the English folk ballad and the King James Bible over the complex and less accessible styles of the twentieth-century modernist writers. Even stranger than his obscure reputation as a poet is the absolute neglect of his two fine and distinguished novels, *Better a Dinner of Herbs* (1950) and *The Hawk and the Sun* (1955). One is always aware in these novels that the writer is a poet. Descriptions are expertly drawn, with a moving lyricism that in only a few words evokes vivid visual images. Each paragraph, each chapter, resonates with a clear and subtle rhythm, and the novels themselves move with a pace and structure uniquely suited to the stories they have to tell.

Like the narratives of many folk tales, the plot of *Better a*

5

Dinner of Herbs is relatively straightforward. A young man named Enid, who has raised his dead sister's child and worked his family's mountain farm all his adult life, decides to sell out and travel to the lowlands. He wants to change his life, and he wants to find love. On the way down from the hills he gives a ride to a woman named Mary returning home to her husband and children after a visit of several weeks with her sister. She and Enid become friends and then lovers. Enid becomes overseer on the farm of her husband, who has abandoned the fields to devote himself to preaching and the private expiation of a sin committed many years before. To divulge more of the plot would violate the reader's pleasure in following the events of the novel to a final conclusion. But the story never grows too complex or urgent. In its slow, careful way it moves inexorably toward an end foreshadowed from the first page.

Reece draws his characters with a few generic strokes. We come to know them fairly well, though in fact we learn little about them, only the essential details. But their lives—spent in the rural mountain and farm lands—are simple and uncluttered. They are like characters from the Old Testament stories, from folk ballads, or from Reece's own poetry. Yet the mythic simplicity of this novel's story contrasts with the rich and evocative way in which Reece chooses to relate it. In structure this novel is not traditional at all.

Reece tells his story in a style distinctly reminiscent of William Faulkner in *The Sound and the Fury* and *As I Lay Dying*. He narrates through the thoughts and emotions of the important characters—Enid, Danny, Jason, the Preacher, and others—but they do not speak to the reader, only to each other, or to themselves. Each chapter reflects a particular personality's way of experiencing and understanding the world. And however much the Mississippi novelist might have influenced the Georgia poet, Reece has written his novel in a way that is distinctly his own. In structure it is simpler and more straightforward than Faulkner's fiction. And its view of human nature is different as well. Faulkner's novels are psychologically introspective, obsessively focused on the inner turmoil of characters struggling to be reconciled to their own personal pasts and regional histories. Reece is also interested in the psychological growth of his characters, but they are not ridden with angst and neurotic confusion. They grapple with those same problems that have plagued human beings for thousands of years: loneliness, desire, love, grief, boredom. Reece's narratives are melancholic, balladic, carefully and quietly meditative. His characters do not fear the world, though often they are unsure of it. They confront it with anticipation, expectancy. These emotions dominate the novel's first half, as Danny and Enid slowly wend their way out of the mountains toward life, the Preacher's farm, and whatever the future might hold.

Unlike Faulkner's rich, baroque, heavily subordinated language, Reece's sentences are clipped, spare, tersely poetic. Each paragraph, each sentence, is a carefully crafted gem. Especially in the novel's first half, the narrative language calls as much attention to itself as it does the events and thoughts it conveys. The opening narrative of Danny's thoughts as he awakens to the morning is a prose poem ("To erupt from sleep into the world of neither night nor morning, in the large old attic close under the rafters. To be in the state of neither waking nor sleeping. To move in the twilight world of first waking . . ."). Many other passages, such as the account of Enid and Danny's journey down from the mountains, the description of the laborers at work in the Preacher's field, and the closing chapter, are equally fine.

Structurally, the novel moves in a circle. We begin on the day following the climactic moment of the story. Then we move back in time, to the farm of Enid and Danny in the mountains and the life they have lived there for years. We next move forward, through Enid's decision to sell the farm, the beginning of his journey with Danny, their meeting with Mary, and their arrival at the Preacher's farm. In the course of this downward movement, which all the while is circling back toward the beginning point, we take occasional side trips, as when Enid recalls the night he discovered his sister Daisy with a lover, the same night on which Danny was conceived, and whose birth caused his sister's death. The novel's movement not only suggests cyclic continuation but also hints at an ultimate destiny that will bind the characters up inextricably with one another and will not be complete until the book's final page. The novel's structure is thus like the structure of memory, the chronicle of each character's effort to know and understand the events that have brought him to where he stands. But even more it is a chronicle, a lyric tribute to the vital texture of experience, the ecstatic apprehension of any given moment as one moves through time toward whatever ultimate end.

Though Reece was known especially as a Georgia poet, in keeping with the nonspecific, folk quality of his language Georgia is never named as the setting of *Better a Dinner of Herbs*, nor are particular North Georgia locations ever identified. It is not even clear that Reece has such specific locations in mind. The setting is simply and indefinitely rural and could exist anywhere. But the mountains of the novel's beginning certainly have the feel of Georgia mountains, and as Danny and Enid move down into the foothills and farmlands, these seem Georgian as well. Yet the novel's setting would probably seem familiar to anyone who grew up in a region where mountains give way to lowlands and farm country. The absence of specific geographical names invests the setting with universality. It is a place familiar to the human heart rather than to any particular regional heritage, a setting better known to imagination, the setting of folklore and of myth.

Reece himself grew up on a farm at the foot of Blood Mountain north of Dahlonega, Georgia, in a time and place where most of the work of farming was done by hand. He never saw a car, one of his biographers tells us, until he reached the age of eight. Even as an adult, in between stints of teaching and writing, he continued to farm. He knew the texture of the hard farming life of the North Georgia mountains well. Perhaps because of this familiarity (a 1945 publicity photograph in the Atlanta *Journal-Constitution* shows him hard at work behind a mule-drawn plow), *Better a Dinner of Herbs* contains some of the most vivid and realistic descriptions of farm labor in American fiction. Even in its realism, however, such a passage as the following is intensely lyrical:

> On a day they went out to the fields. The air was heavy and sultry and a few clouds lay lengthwise across the lower border of the sky. The rows of corn in that field ran east and west and the first light slanted from the long green blades of the corn. As they moved westward it rippled and fell from the rumps of the mules the plowers followed to the cultivators. Toward noon the sky was overcast, the wind blew faintly, scarcely stirring the still corn whose broad dark blades were spotted with light, as if part of them were in the shade and a part in the sun, yet there was no sun and by this sign they knew it would rain as certainly as if the drops were pattering already upon the blades.

Reece's novel is about people who work the land, measuring out their lives by the turn of the seasons and the success or failure of the harvest. In this sense it reminds us of such books as Willa Cather's *My Antonia* or John Steinbeck's *The Grapes of Wrath* or Faulkner's *The Hamlet*. Yet better and more intimately than these writers, Reece knew what it was to till the soil, to guide a mule-drawn plow, to sweat and labor in seemingly endless monotony beneath the hot summer Georgia sun. The rhythms and rituals of farming, the closeness of men and women to the land on which they depend, to the natural world which can save or destroy them, are deeply embedded in this novel.

Perhaps it is appropriate then that Reece's novel has no real ending in the traditional sense. Relationships that have lasted a lifetime dissolve, and others that seem on the verge of maturity pass away entirely. One character finds a home and a family. Another wanders off and never returns. Yet we know that their lives do not close with the novel's conclusion. This is not the happy ending of popular romance, but it is not a sad ending either. Instead it is a sort of half-conclusion, an end that is a beginning, or at the least a continuation, a stoic acquiescence to the vagaries of life and whatever it might bring.

1992

BETTER A DINNER OF HERBS

PART 1
TO WAKE

I

DANNY

To wake in that house.

To erupt from sleep into the world of neither night nor morning, in the large old attic close under the rafters. To be in the state of neither waking nor sleeping. To move in the twilight world of first waking when sounds are blurred on their edges and the eyes are filmed with the dross of sleep. There was still only darkness. Danny could see nothing except a few faint stars in the field of the north window. But moment by moment the sky was brightening with the sloughing off of night. The air was sucking at the first straws of the sun.

Without let or hindrance he would imitate the coming to life of day. He would shed the film of sleep like a snake its old skin in the summer meadow and move fresh and alive into the world of waking. He would emerge from the cocoon of sleep and spread his mind in the sun of consciousness. He was hearing the first sounds, the usual sounds of morning. The rooster crew in the lot by the barn, a loud and imperious sound. The cow bawled for her morning roughage. There were sounds below stairs, blurred and indistinct. There was never any accounting for the sounds below stairs because they depended on the movements of humans, and there was never any telling when these creatures of impulse and free will would be hustling about. It might be on one errand at one moment and on another the next. Never the same errands, never the same movements at the same time morning after morning. The cow bawled for her roughage and it was six o'clock. But the Preacher did not bawl for his breakfast. He rose and clattered about, building a fire, and then the sound of his wife, of Mary, would join his sounds—but was it four or six or seven? It was anybody's guess.

That was the way it usually was, but as he listened he was aware that something was missing from the sounds of the morning, from the outside morning where the light grew like the glow of a brush fire against the night, spreading great and red and wonderful in the east.

The cow bawled again and there was the twitter of fowl and the long, low whistle of a bird in the thicket to the west of the house, but the mare did not neigh.

The Preacher's mare.

Yesterday. . . .

He was not yet out of sleep. It clung in wisps to this thinking. The fog of sleep in the crags of the mind. The indistinct landscape of the mind. I am lost in this valley, there is fog here. He turned onto his back and his hands lay open, palms down, on his thighs.

This is my body. I am warm. This is myself. He was well pleased that he was himself. Of course he was himself. Who else would he be . . . except the stranger that lived in his skull in the night, in his sleep? The stranger with wings, or flight without wings. The wonders of the night-born stranger.

He was himself; and perfectly still he waited for the flood of light from the one north window to drive the darkness through the cracks of the floor and expose the three beds with their humps of sleepers, the crazy checks of the covers growing clumps of hair, dark and light and dark, the three heads besides his own.

The stars left the north window. The eyes of the house except this one looked onto the ground. That was because they were all on the first floor with no height to look from. The west windows looked over the barnyard to the mountains beyond. The eastern windows looked on the road and across a valley given over to fields, to where the sight was stopped by another mountain lying roughly parallel to the mountain in the west. The south windows looked up the road as it emerged from the blind southeast corner of the house; and the north window on the first floor looked over the creek in the distance, curving like a crooked index finger around the base of the mountain blocking the valley to the north.

But the upstairs window looked at the sky. Like the eye of Polyphemus it stared into the bright north. Morning entered first by this window and, finding itself above stairs, creaked and settled under the thrust of the sun until it reached the floor below. There was light at the window, but it was ghost-colored, whey-colored light. The quilts had not yet grown their fronds of hair.

He moved with the languid motion of the newly wakened and his knee touched a warmth and softness not of himself. He was sleeping with the Idiot. Because, he being twelve, his wishes were less to be heeded than a man's or a sixteen-year-old boy's he slept with the Idiot. The Idiot was asleep still. The pure peace of sleep was upon his face. He knew it from before. Time and again since he and his Uncle Enid had come to dwell here and he to sleep with him he had raised himself upon his elbows or lain on his belly with his hands cupped about his chin and looked at the sleeping Idiot. He was beautiful.

But you do not like to touch the Idiot. You are troubled about the senseless boy because he is like a cheat, a thing that is not what it pretends to be; he is not sealed with the indivisible seal of entity. A mermaid in a book. Fish and woman and slippery-slick with scales. Yet there is nothing so fascinating as the Idiot. He lies sleeping with the pure peace of sleep upon his face, and he will waken and there will be no cloud upon his countenance for he does not wake to trouble. What does he wake to? To a clapping of hands, to a taste of bread and a continual bleating of joy.

I don't want to sleep with the Idiot.

He is warm and soft. He is like an animal. He is not in his head. I don't want to hurt him. Once I slapped him in the face. There was pain in my body from slapping him. It was a good pain but the Idiot only looked at me while the red from the blow of my hand went out of his face, and then he clapped his hands together and sang out, "Boodle, boodle, boodle!" There is no use to hurt the Idiot.

I sleep with the Idiot because Jason will not sleep with him. Jason is his brother. If I had a brother that was not in his head I would have to sleep with him. Uncle Enid sleeps in the bed nearest the window. It is the best bed. If Jason slept with the Idiot there would not be room for me. I would like to sleep with Jason.

Waking is in the sea, in a rough sea. The swimmer is toward the shore and in the troughs is consciousness but the waves are sleep. While the light grew in the window the waves were over him and Danny swam in the sea. He emerged on the shore of waking still half drowned and the oblong of window light startled him. It was in the wrong place.

This is not the house. This is the house I was brought to by Uncle Enid. In our own house I slept in a room by a hall and across the hall Uncle Enid slept in his own bed. The window is wrong. It is in the side of the house that stands to the east and the light comes in across my feet and not into my face. That is in our house.

He was on the shore and the waters of that sea from which he had emerged dripped slowly from him. The sounds of the outside morning came to him again. The bawling of the cow continued; the rooster crew again and there was the sound of other fowls, the slow and happy conversing, the chir-chir-

chiring of the hens in the yard. He was impatient for the missing sound. What it was escaped him in the second immersion in sleep, but he remembered again suddenly. The mare did not neigh for her feed. The spirited mare did not neigh and nicker in an imperious and demanding voice for the Preacher to come and give her corn and a forkful of hay.

He lay listening for the mare, and he heard the sound of many. The sound was continuous and blurred but now and then elements of the little thunder he heard coming from the direction of the barn flew free and were sounds of hoofs upon hard ground and frequent nickerings, as of many horses tethered and moving to the ends of their tethers in one direction and back again, nickering all the while at each other. He could not account for a congress of horses, and his half-sleeping reason told him it was playing a trick upon him, from the source of his imagination supplying an over-supply of the sound he listened for.

Someone went from the door and through the gate between the house and the barn that closed itself because of weights hung on a wire from the unhinged edge to a peg set in the ground at an angle from the supporting post. It was not the Preacher who had gone through the gate on his way to feed the mare. He always closed the gate carefully and without fuss save for a little sound the weights made falling against each other, the alto clink of the old plow against the broken wedge and the bass clank of the wedge against the wagon thimble that hung from the wire. Whoever passed through the gate now let it swing to freely and the weights set up a clanging that reverberated in a jelly of sound.

Because the sounds except one were right the window was right.

Good morning. I am myself. I was in the Other House but I am in this house. The quilts have grown their hair. The dark

hair next the window is my Uncle Enid's. His face is toward
the window. I cannot see his face. What is in his face? He is
swapping his face. It is not like it used to be. His hair is his
own and his forehead under his hair. His eyes are the stranger's.
He. Where will he go? I will be left. I will be left if the stranger
goes but he is not a stranger. He is my Uncle Enid.

Jason.

Jason's hair is the color of straw. You cannot tell it from his
face in this light. He is asleep still. His face is good when he
is asleep. When he is awake his face is good if he smiles. He is
full of fury. He is gentle like a cat. I run from Jason but I
want to run toward him. He will tousle me till it hurts.

Ezra is beside me. He is the Idiot. I touched him awhile ago
with my knee. I was startled when I touched him. He is warm,
he is like an animal. He is blond like a rabbit's belly. He will
pop up from being asleep. He will sit up suddenly and be
awake and he will pivot his legs from under the cover and run
down the stairs.

But I was in the Other House. It was good there. I remember from the Other House. I slept in my own room there and
Uncle Enid. . . . Who is downstairs? There are more women
than Mary and the Old Woman downstairs.

The sounds came drifting through the floor of the attic.
They came up blurred and indistinct, except now for the clear
high-pitched sound of wailing. The sound of wailing came up
distinctly. It came up as if it mounted by the stairs and was at
the head of the stairs, poised there, shaking the attic air. He
came sharp awake. He heard the sound and remembered. The
congregation below stairs and the congress of horses were accounted for as he remembered the events of the day before.

He wanted to touch Jason or Uncle Enid for protection
against the sound. But he lay with the Idiot in the crook of his

body while the sound of wailing came to him, punctuated by the beating of his own heart and another measured sound: the bong-bonging of the clock on the mantel below as it struck seven.

2

UNCLE ENID

Before he awoke Uncle Enid had three dreams.

In the first he did not know where he was. The gray stuff was formless and void, like fog unstirred by the wind. He stood for a moment looking up as if waiting for a command. Then he thrust his hands into the gray stuff and began to climb.

It was not hard at first. There were projections he could grasp with his hands and when he pulled himself up his feet found ledges and crevices as if they knew of themselves where to probe for them. He went upward hand over hand.

He climbed through the gray stuff. It whirled and eddied but never broke. It wavered slowly and made convolutions but never once broke so he could see the face of the cliff on which he climbed.

It was growing more difficult. The muscles of his legs were beginning to strain in thrusting his weight upward. His biceps bulged with the effort of drawing the weight of his body from one handhold to the next.

There were weights to his feet; they were secured with cords and dangled below him out of sight in the gray stuff of the void. He did not know what the weights were but they were going to drag him from the face of the cliff. He felt the tremors of fatigue going in a continuous shiver through his muscles. He strained to lift the weights from one foothold to the next. He clung frantically to the cliff.

He came to a ledge wide enough on which to stand. He clung with his left hand and lifted his feet, one after the other, and unloosed the knots of the cords that bound the weights to him. They fell soundlessly into the void. Considering the drag the weights had had upon him the knots that bound them to his feet were surprisingly easy to untie.

Afterward he began to climb again, at first with the ease he had experienced on first starting out. As he progressed up the cliff through the void he felt the pull of the weights upon him again. He had to stop and free himself of them at intervals as long as he climbed. There was no end to the cliff and he climbed in the gray void and was glad. If the cliff had stopped it would have been the end of everything.

There was a subtle shift in the weather of the dream.

He stood with his hand on the lever that springs the trap of the scaffold his grandfather saw in the war. The head of the deserter was hidden in a black hood and his whole figure was dark and indistinct in the early morning light. The faces of the men ranged around the scaffold were stern and unforgiving, but they were not looking at the deserter. They were looking at him. He stood with his hand on the lever and the order came to spring the trap and he began to push it forward slowly. The deserter was no longer standing on the scaffold. Someone else had taken his place. The new figure on the trap was smaller than the deserter, he was probably twelve years old. His shanks were thin and immature under his thin clothing. The boy wore no mask but his back was toward him. He could not see his face. He pushed the lever forward and the boy hurtled through the trap of the scaffold but he was not brought up short of the ground. There had been no rope around his neck. The figures by the scaffold began to laugh; they laughed in raucous and disjointed bursts of laughter while the dream faded.

Immediately, or so it seemed in the dream, he was in the house where he was born. He came in through the door carrying something in his hand.

"What is it?" his mother said, which was strange, for she had been dead for the better part of eight years.

"I don't know," he said, "it was given to me on the road." He stood holding the object, looking for a place in the room where he might set it down.

"It is valuable, and it will break if I drop it," he said to his mother. "I don't know what it is. I'll set it here on the mantel."

"Be careful," his mother said, "you will drop it."

"No," he said, "I'll set it here on the mantel." He released his hold on the object. He thought it was resting on the mantel. But his mother was screaming. He glanced sharply at his mother. She was staring fascinated at the object as it fell. He looked toward the place where he had set the object. There was no mantel there. He was disconcerted. He looked at his empty hands and his mother screamed as if in the object she were suffering an irredeemable loss.

In the second dream, or the second phase of the first dream, for he had not awakened, he sensed even in sleep that his memory was being spelled out to him like a recitation by another of a song or a speech he had memorized himself.

But this is a dream, part of his brain said, speaking to the other part of his brain that insisted the dream wore the cloak of truth.

He was in the Other House, where he was born. It was dark because a quilt had been hung over the window to shut out the light. Was it to hide that the window was darkened? It was hot. He was sweating. If the quilt were not there the outside air would move through the window and cool the room. If there is nothing to hide why not remove the quilt? No. The window was darkened because there was death in the room.

He had been expecting it.

He was at work in the field. The sweat ran in trickles down his back and cascaded from his eyebrows into his eyes. The world was still and bright and fiery in the blaze of a July noon. He rested between the plow handles behind the mare. Sweat traced little rivers down the legs of the mare and dripped into the damp new-plowed ground between the corn rows. The blades of the corn waved a little at the height of the mare's back, they moved a little to the wind that came through them, diluted by each row of corn as it crossed the field. The wind was as active as a young pup in the sedge at the field's edge. By the time it reached him it was like the warm and fetid breath of a dying animal.

As if it were the appointed time for her to come he looked up and saw Old Nance, his mother's friend, hurrying toward him from the road. She came with her old ambling gait toward him down a corn row. He began to unhitch the traces. It seemed that he would faint from the heat and lie on the cool earth where the plow had turned up the dampness that dwelt below the surface of the soil. He would escape the news bearer from the road. Old Nance, Old Nance who had been with his mother lying sick in her room. But he took the mare by the bridle and met her on the way.

"Hurry, hurry!" she said.

He nodded without speaking. As an afterthought he reached his hand toward the old woman and gave her the mare's reins. His stride grew and grew as he made haste toward his own house. He broke into a run.

His mother lay in her own room. She lay on her back and her mouth was open and she labored through it a little breath at heartbreaking intervals. Her face was white, as if the chalk of the bone had penetrated the flesh and was freed already from its long bondage as an element in the frame of life. A fly shrilled in the window behind the quilt. Through the dimness of the room he could see that her eyes were open and also that her mind was not at home in its house. He looked through the window of her eyes and noted with grief that the inhabitant was gone out of her mind's house.

He stood by the bed without speaking.

A second of his mother's friends, Miss Mitchie, scarcely less wrecked by time than the figure on the bed, stood at the head of the bed and moved the turkey-wing fan back and forth, her free arm resting on her little round belly, her eyes grave, contemplative and grave.

"I said before you come," she said, "I said to myself, she is dying and not a man soul on the place. I fan away the flies and the heat and Nance runs to fetch her son."

"Hush," he said, "you are talking foolishly."

"I am not talking foolishly," she said with a touch of anger. "I said to myself, when she was a child she gazed into her father's face and when she was older she carried her lover's image in her heart as in a locket. When she conceived she required her husband, but she is dying and not a man soul on the place. She can die without men."

"Hush," he said.

"That's what I said to myself," she said. She stood impassive as a stone in the field, her hand moving the fan back and forth in a rhythm as inexorable as the rhythm of cycling time.

Their eyes were on the cover but if it rose and fell at all it was with a motion so imperceptible it could not be seen. The fly ceased its shrilling behind the quilt. The fan paused in Miss Mitchie's hand. The room was still as if all things in it had conspired together toward cessation.

Then his mother spoke.

"Son," she said.

His knees almost buckled under him, for he foresaw in that moment all the wounds of his spirit running with anguish where the fibers of her being had been torn from it like nerves from the living flesh.

He did not answer a word but took the hand that lay dead and without will on the cover. It was drained already of warmth, but the eyes became inhabited at his touch and their living light sent illumination into the room.

"Why is there no light?" she said. "Is it day?" He knew she was questioning to establish in her mind whether it was the darkness of night she saw or that other darkness.

"Yes," he said. And he wondered that the living always made the rooms of the dying shadowed. Was it to acquaint the dying with darkness? They are too soon acquainted. Do they shut out the light upon the act of death to erase the image of the dying from their minds forever? Must the dead go faceless into death? Are they without visage before their flesh is wrecked in corruption? Let them behold the light. Let the dying look upon light as they go forth, their flight be as a bird's traversing the arc of sky lit with the morning sun.

He unhooked the quilt from the window and the light lay across her face and the warmth of the sun was in it.

"I will dwell in the minds of those that love me," she said, her voice faint, "I will dwell in Beulah and in the dust and in the minds of those that love me. In this face I will live. My hands were done when I was a grown woman but my face was as dough kneaded by the hands of the Lord. When I was a child I was joyful and in my face was joy. Has not my face been the countenance of love? I am old and in my face is the sum of my sorrows. Look in my face to read the tally of all my tears."

She was breathless with effort. The fanner moved her hand back and forth over her face and the little wind of its passing moved the stray strands of gray hairs on her forehead.

"Where is the child?" she said and he had a momentary vision of the young Danny playing outside, playing by himself, unaware of the meaning of death or its very existence.

"Outside," he said, and he meant to ask if he should call him but she would not give him time. She was impatient to have it finished.

"You will keep the child," she said, looking at him so that he could make no reservations in his eyes.

"You will love the child," she said next after he had promised, and it was not a question but a commandment.

"Yes, yes," he said, looking at the face that suddenly became strange as if it put off for the first time the marks of all care and arranged its lineaments into the mask of peace it would wear for eternity.

And she dwelt in Beulah and in the dust and in the minds of those that loved her.

He was gone out of that house but the dream continued. He was climbing in the gray void again. It was easy at first but as he progressed the weights were upon him again to hinder his progress. Before he was compelled to stop and remove them one foot was mysteriously freed of its weight. It had fallen from him, of course, because the cord that bound it to him was broken.

Afterward he climbed upward one foot fettered and one free. It was easier than pulling both weights but it occurred to him that he was still hobbled, like a convict.

He rested in a suspension of the dream. The dream was not dissolved but he; he was pure and free in the void of gray nothing. There were no objects in the void, nothing moved there. He was free in the edgeless sea of gray nothing.

But he was drawing close to something again. The gray mass of nothing began to dissolve and he saw that he was standing on a plank several feet from the ground. The inverted V of his own barn roof came out of the grayness and hung over his head. He reached out and steadied himself with one hand against the wall of the barn.

This is a high place. I could fall. Down. But I am safe. I am holding to something, to the studding of the scaffold. It is in the crook of my left arm. The plank on which I am standing is too long and if I should let my weight rest on it beyond the support that reaches from the barn wall to the studding it would overbalance and hurtle me to the ground. But I am perfectly safe. I am a little dizzy but that is the way high places affect me. I do not like high places. But if the plank should overbalance? My end of the plank is all right. The pressure is on the other end of the plank. I feel the urge of pressure against the sole of my foot. The bone of my leg resists the pressure and it bends the fulcrum of my knee, and my knee resists and my hip resists. I am holding my own with the damn fool plank. It must be crazy to act this way.

In the dream he looked toward the far end of the plank. Danny had ventured too far toward his end and the weight of his body was serving to carry the plank down. Danny must have asked to be allowed on the scaffold to hand him nails while he repaired the weatherboarding under the eaves. Danny was not looking at him. He was looking beyond and a little to the side. He was looking toward the south pasture and he had not yet discovered his peril.

I could transfer my weight from this end of the plank. . . . Even in dream he rebelled against the inference pointed by the suggestion of his sleeping mind, but his knee ceased to resist the pressure exerted on the plank by Danny's body. Danny's dream face suddenly flashed him a startled look as he felt the plank falling away from under him. He was hunching his body forward from the waist and raising his arms like the wings of a picked bird in an effort to regain his lost balance; and even as he tried in sleep to determine whether he dreamed or remembered the dream switched suddenly and he was again in the weather of the first dream.

For the third time he was climbing up the cliff face. He was climbing nimbly for he had lost the weight from his other foot also. At the rate he was climbing he must surely reach the top soon.

And the third dream:

He stood and disputed with a stranger over the possession of a thing both of them claimed. The landscape was indeterminate, he thought he had never seen it before but the feeling of unfamiliarity the landscape bred within him might have been due to the oddness of the light. It was leaden gray. It filtered through the trees with a visible motion and gave the air about them where they disputed on the road the appearance of night. But it was not night. The shape of the sun was plainly discernible where it floated just over the tops of the trees, a cloudy and baleful eye, and from time to time the two of them, he and the stranger, glanced at it as if to see if it had yet observed them in what they did.

The object over which they disputed was itself indistinct, wrapped in gray cloth or folded in the gray folds of that leaden air. Its exact identity was not revealed to them during the course of the quarrel, though they must have been able to remove the veil of its wrappings and expose it if they had but tried. It seemed that by keeping it hidden each would add to the validity of his claim of ownership.

Neither of them possessed the object in fee simple as one owns a knife or an acre of land or even the living organism that is a dog, or a horse. The stranger seemed to have a written claim upon it but could not produce it; and it would have been invalid if he had, for both of them recognized that the object of the dispute had a will of its own. Therefore it could invalidate any claim by willing to do so. An acre of land cannot say: I will not be possessed, so it is easy to establish a claim upon it. In a contest where wills are pitted one against the other there is no victory. It is only when two wills are in harmony, as in love, that one can make a claim upon another. And the perpetuation of the claim depends upon the perpetuation of the harmony.

So the object had a will of its own and each apparently had a claim upon it.

"It is mine," said the stranger.

"No," he said, "it is mine."

"Tell me a thing that will prove it is yours," said the stranger.

"I want it," he said.

That was good reasoning, he thought, and the stranger did not disagree by saying that was no proof. Instead he countered with the equally valid claim that he wanted it too.

That was an impasse, and so they stood for a moment in the falling gray air, and then the stranger said,

"Tell me another thing to prove that it is yours."

He stood a moment, thinking, and then he said,

"I will call it, and if it comes to me that will prove that it is mine." He called, and looked toward the folded gray object as if he expected it to come to him as a dog would respond to a whistle from the lips of his master. But it remained in the same attitude as when they first began to dispute. It did not move in the wavering gray air.

He was a little astonished that it did not respond. "You call it and see if it is yours," he said to the stranger, disturbed by the thought that it might be neither's.

"No," the stranger said. "If *I* called it and it did not come you would take that as proof that it is yours and not mine."

Some time passed while they stood in the leaden-gray air and argued. And then he became aware that the object was closer to him than when they first began to dispute. He felt good about this, as if a dog he had called had been wary and fearful, even distrustful to a certain extent, but in the end responded to his coaxing and came all the same.

He pointed out to the stranger that the object had approached him and was closer to him than to the stranger, which had not been the case when they first began to dispute. But this only made the stranger all the more determined to have the object for himself, and they began to dispute in anger.

Suddenly it occurred to him that if he was to possess the object he must dispose of the stranger and by so doing invalidate his claim to ownership. How this was to be accomplished seemed simple in that gray air.

He pretended to lose interest in the object and began coaxing and beguiling the stranger, trying to persuade him to trust him near his person, but the stranger would not be persuaded. He kept the same distance between them as when they first began to dispute, would not let it lessen by so much as an inch.

It was in his mind to kill the stranger. The contemplated act did not seem monstrous and the object had somehow communicated the feeling that it approved. They were moving along the road in the gray air, and they kept their relative positions, and the object its relative position, a little closer now to him than to the stranger.

He began to cast about for some means of bringing his intention to kill the stranger to fulfillment and as he did so a conviction of the necessity of stealth came over him. He must perform the act without anyone knowing he did it, else he would surely lose the object of the dispute and perhaps suffer other dire consequences besides. The object's approval could not be publicly expressed; the approval was tacit and once the deed was published abroad it would have to renounce him for his act.

He looked all about him but there was no one to be seen; nothing moved in the surrounding gray landscape except the visible air. He raised the club, a stick he had picked up from under one of the trees, and aimed a blow at the stranger, for somehow he had come within striking distance of him. But just before the club struck against the skull of the stranger he disappeared. He vanished like smoke into the gray air. He was overcome with a feeling of wrath because he had been thwarted, but then it struck him that since the stranger had disappeared he could not press his claim of ownership of the disputed object. He turned with all his longing for the object to possess it, but it was gone too.

When he discovered the object of the dispute was gone as well as the stranger his wrath grew in intensity until it rose like a shriek through the dull throbbing of his brain. But he still felt the need for secrecy, and he looked about to see if there had been witnesses but he saw nothing but the baleful eye of the cloudy-silver sun, and a hawk wheeling in the eldritch air.

He shifted into the preceding dream again. He saw Danny as he was about to fall from the tilting board. Danny was looking straight into his eyes and besides the surprise and the beginning of terror that crowded in his look he read there the heartbreaking appeal of one who asks help and knows the asking is in vain because it is not in the power of the one besought to render it.

But it was in his power. He stopped the board in its tilt by transferring his weight to the foot upon the board. And the weight of his conscience thrust against the board, and the power of the thrust was doubled and trebled and multiplied by another incalculable weight:

That was the weight of love.

Yet again he climbed in the gray void and one foot bore its weight. He reached the top of the cliff this time and looked over. And his eyes were blinded by an illumination like the light of a thousand suns. He would have been destroyed, but at the moment he looked over the cliff top he was not himself but another man.

And then he woke.

He glanced about the attic, still vague in the early morning light. His nephew was awake and lying on his left side, looking at Jason in the bed between them. He could not tell whether Jason woke or slept, whether he was communing with his nephew without words, as he often did, or with the silence and forgetfulness of sleep. A lament for Danny began in his heart. The tears fell in his heart for the boy, his nephew, lost to him by the curious circumstance that the identity of his father had been revealed after the passing of thirteen years.

The clock was striking. He heard the last three bongs as it struck in a series that began in mystery and did not tell him the time, since the three terminal notes might have signified any three hours of the twelve circled about the clock's face. And he heard another sound, the sound of wailing that ascended by the stairs.

He glanced covertly at his nephew and hated suddenly the boy Jason in the bed between them because the two were brothers. The tears fell in his heart as he rose, avoiding Danny's eyes, and descended the stairs to the first floor where the Preacher lay dead in the northwest corner of the largest room.

3

JASON

Jason awoke.

Without any movement except opening his eyes he awoke and lay on his side looking at Danny in the bed opposite with his still, shut stare. He did not know what woke him. He had sprung from sleep into full waking instantly. As a trout's leap carries it from the depth arching above the surface of the water, so he plunged upward from sleep into the upper strata of waking. He did not know what had released the spring that flung him through that transition, in that pause of time too infinitesimal to measure. He heard the sounds below stairs, but for the moment they had no meaning, existed as entities without cause or relation, sealed in a vacuum of time without beginning or end.

The literal light lay in the attic, in it the shine of leaves and the comfort of the twittering birds between leaf and leaf in every tree it shone over. Yet he felt vaguely uneasy, as if a menace lay in his mind. In what direction? If he could pursue the light and not the disbodied sounds that came to him he might avoid, or even by-pass, whatever the menace to his happiness might be. He lay perfectly still and looked at Danny with his still, shut stare.

The light in Danny's face, not Danny. He is always asking with his eyes. He is at a gate and won't come through until somebody asks him. Is he waiting for me to ask him? Through what gate? He saw in Danny's eyes all that he was, or might be, to him. He was not ready to open a gate. He was not willing to surrender the secret and inviolate core of his being to anyone. Unbreached the walls of the fortress that was himself stood beyond a moat of fury and harshness.

I will not ask him.

Yet he was lonely and sometimes terrified in the fortress of himself.

He looked out along the literal light to the outside world. With his back to the window and the light coming over his shoulder he saw outside the fluffy red hens that chir-chirred in the yard, and the cow with her great patient eyes standing in her stall, waiting. There are two worlds. There is the world outside and the world in my head. Things happen inside me. I am a house. I am a house like one I saw pictured in a book. It is full of rooms and windows and there is nobody in the house except myself. The outside world does not matter. In the outside world the animals move about and do not look at you. They are busy with their own affairs. I remember the fox with his nose to the ground and his tail like a slinking dog's behind him. He moved in the brush. He glanced at me and went on about his business. Nothing happened to me with the fox's passing. I was the same when he was out of sight. Other people are houses. Nobody comes out of the door of one house and goes into the door of the other.

I will not ask Danny.

I remember Danny. I remember he was standing up in the wagon and I had never seen him before. He was with my mother and the man in the wagon. He jumped from the wagon and stood looking at me. He is always looking at me. He knows what I want without my telling him.

I remember the fox.

But the fox doesn't matter. I am shut up in my house. I would like sometimes for someone to come in and visit me. I don't know how to let them in. I know some who have been in my house. I don't know how they got in. They got in by chance and I put them out again. They wanted to see what was in the house. They wanted to see and go tell. Like going to the house of somebody who is poor and telling what you saw there. The poor people would hate you for it. They didn't come for shelter nor to share.

But he knows what I want without my telling him. Once I wanted him to go outside and play with me at the haystacks. The haystacks are good. They smell like the first thing in the morning. And I looked at him and he knew what I wanted and he went out after me. It was like having a pup on a string. When I would be sitting on one side of the house and him on the other and I would look at him and we would rise and go out the others looked at each other and smiled. They did that when my pup learned to stand on his hind legs. We were like a dog that is good at tricks.

He stirred and stretched himself and felt the flow of his muscles like waves under his skin. He was somehow aroused by the feel of his muscles flowing under his palms and he looked at Danny thinking, will I ask him?

But Danny was gone out of himself. He was looking directly at him without seeing him at all. There was a difference in his gaze. As if the sky that had always been clear had suddenly assumed a cloud.

He is not there. He is out of his house.

He was puzzled and a little hurt that for the first time he could remember Danny had shut him out of his eyes. And he was puzzled at the hurt. It was light, it fell upon his spirit lightly, like a play blow delivered in a pantomime of fisticuffs.

He would take no notice of it.

Yet Danny who usually saw him only was looking at him without seeing him at all, and he felt a sudden need to re-establish himself in Danny's eyes. He raised himself on his elbow and looked directly at Danny, and when he saw that he was the subject of such attention he smiled and the asking returned to his clear eyes.

He allowed his still, shut stare to soften and enclose Danny. It was as if he had opened a gate for him, and when he had passed through closed it again behind him. For a moment they stared into each other's eyes and then Danny, distracted by the noise below stairs, was gone out of himself again. But what passed between them was not forgotten. It left them each a little shaken, as if they had made contact across a dangerous chasm.

His mind was wrenched from Danny to his father. Perhaps it was a sound he did not consciously apprehend that set the shuttle of his mind flying about his father. My father with a whip in his hand. It was not for the mare. He was good to the mare. It sang in the air and stang like bees under my shirt. I heard it swish and swish and the feeling left my back and then blood began to seep through my shirt. It ran down my arm where the whip had touched the muscle of my arm and left it without feeling, hanging like a rotten limb from a tree.

I don't want to remember that about my father. He is without his face in the room downstairs. That is why.

So he had to recognize the sounds below stairs. He was aware of the wailing and had been for some time, and of the sounds of people moving about, going in and out the doors. It was his mother who was weeping below stairs. He could see in his mind how she knelt by the side of the shrouded figure and announced her loss in the fearful and somehow unwholesome language of grief that has prospered since sorrow began in the world.

But I didn't cry. His eyes were crazy and he swung his free hand back from his body, behind him to give force to the other hand holding the whip. He got angrier with each blow but I didn't cry. I had to force my mouth to stay shut and the muscles bunched under my chin and I could feel my heart beating there, like the pulse you can see in a frog's throat. He was angry because I didn't cry.

We were far apart. Even when we were close to each other, in presence I mean, we were far apart. I kept wanting to shout when I talked to him because he seemed so far off I was afraid he couldn't hear me.

I had forgot all about it. He told me to mend the pasture fence where the cows had got through to the corn but I forgot all about it. Until I saw him riding in I had. And then it was too late. I didn't fix the fence, I said, I. . . . And that was when he reached for the whip.

But I won't remember. My mother she said what's the matter with you but I couldn't tell her. I didn't cry but when I began to talk to her the words changed to sobs and they filled my throat and choked me. I ran out of the house.

There was a numb feeling in his brain while he thought about his father. He could see him far off, as if on the far side of a field where he walked a course parallel to his own on the near side of the field. They were so far apart a call would not carry over the gap between them. If he made any effort to move closer to him his father moved away, keeping a distance between them. For a long time he saw this vision swimming in the morning light that came into the attic and flowed over his shoulder.

I put my finger to the blood that ran down my arm and touched it to my tongue. It tasted like salty water. It tasted like brass. He should have told me. I didn't know what to do to please him. If I could have pleased him then he would have smiled at me and it would have been all right. Then I wouldn't have had the tight feeling in my chest. It was tight in my chest, like waiting for the next clap in a thunderstorm.

What's the matter with you, she said. But if I loosened the

muscles of my throat the sobs came out. I ran out of the house. I was going to the barn but Abner was there. He was there in the hall and I went into the woods. I stood by a tree and looked at the ground until when I loosened the muscles of my throat nothing came out and I was all right then.

That must have been the time of the fox. But I was no different when the fox went by. The fox doesn't matter. If Danny was a fox. Something happened to me when he looked at me awhile ago. We went there together.

No son of mine is going to be caught there he said when I asked him. Why I said. What's wrong with it. Do I have to stand here all day and tell you what you know perfectly well already he said. You are not going. But we went anyway. We slipped out of the house and I said be careful and don't make any noise. I didn't want the bees on my back again. When we got there they were dancing.

But I won't think about that.

I wish she wouldn't cry. Every time it starts at the bottom of my stomach and tears all the way up. If she wouldn't cry there wouldn't be the pain in me. He pitied his mother. In his mind he saw her on her usual duties, making her slow and easy progress about the house. He saw her full face, calm and unanxious. He felt the whole force of her large calm being standing between him and homelessness. It was only because of her that the tightness ever left his chest. Only in her undisturbed presence could he relax from his father.

He was almost asleep again. The sounds swam into each other and joined the convolutions of light about his bed, about his head and bursting the roof from the attic so he could look up into the sky that whirled with light. Somewhere in the sounds were the sounds of fiddles and guitars and the thin plinky sounds of a mandolin. These sounds alternated with silence and with a roaring that was like the sound of the wind.

That must have been when we got there. We stood a little back from the house and looked in through the window before we went in. They were dancing. The men on one side of the house and the women on the other, and then a man began to call and they pranced toward each other in the center of the room and bowed and pranced backward to where they started from. You couldn't hear the music good and it looked silly to be prancing there in the silence. When they pranced together the second time they paired off and began to whirl around and around. Their hips jiggled and it looked sillier than the prancing and bowing. It looked like they were. But Danny pulled at my sleeve and said move over I can't see them. Let's go back he said when he had looked and not go in. Come on, let's go back. No I said. He may get the whip to me and I'm going to see it good.

We went in then. We stood by the wall with the other kids and looked at them dancing. It didn't seem silly then because what they were doing fitted with the music. It all went together like the flow and the sound of a creek and it was good.

Well, well, somebody said, here's the Preacher's boy! I wished he hadn't said that because my chest wasn't tight. When he said that my chest was tight again. I tried listening to what the fiddle told them to do on the floor. But it wasn't any good after that. A girl took me by the hand and said I'll show you how and we went whirling and bowing in and out among the others but I couldn't make my feet fit the music. I nearly could. Sometimes for a minute or two they fitted and it was better than anything. And then it would be all wrong again and the music did one thing and my feet did another. You'll learn the girl said. She was breathing hard because it was hard work doing what the music said. It was easy to do what the man who was calling the dance said. You watched the others and did what they did when the man called a figure. But you had to find out inside yourself what the music was telling you to do.

You'll get a tanning when the Preacher finds out about this, somebody said. I didn't say anything, but the tightness in my chest hurt. He won't know nothing about it somebody else said. He won't be around to find out his boy's here. But it was no good after that because my chest was too tight. If you tell I said to Danny on the way home and I took his neck between my finger and thumb and pressed hard until he cried out.

The literal light came through the window and fell over his shoulder. The sound of his mother weeping came up from below and was like a presence in the attic. He hunched himself lower in the bed to escape the weeping and the cover blocked the light from the window so that his face was in twilight. He was falling asleep again. He was able to think that the night was not over and he had been dreaming and presently he would wake to the usual day and everything would be all right again. He would wake and rise and make Danny rise too and go out in the fields and help Abner with whatever he was doing in the field.

An image of the great Abner moved through his mind. He was walking along the path that led from the far field to one near the house. The path was through the woods, parallel to the road but on a higher level. He was walking along the road and he saw Abner coming toward him but on the path. His great bulk loomed over him, mountainous and dark, as they came even with each other. He meant to ask Abner what he planned to do in the field that day, but the figure had changed, it was not Abner but his father coming to meet him on the path, a bloody mass of broken flesh where his face should be. He stared at the flesh dripping blood like tears from the ruined eyes, and he could not bear the sight of it and his knees buckled under him and as he fell he screamed.

His own voice screaming jangled in his ears and he woke fully and lay listening. There were no sounds for a moment below stairs. As the echoes of his scream died a silence possessed the whole household. Those below were poised listening to see if the eerie sound would repeat itself and reveal its source and identity. They were shaken by the unexpected sound out of the composure they had worked all night to perfect in the presence of death. He was a little ashamed of having screamed even though he had been dozing. He saw again the image of his father that had shaken him out of sleep. The image did not fade as he came to full consciousness. Nothing he could think would drive it from his mind. He lay pushing at the image, trying to force it away but there was no hope.

His father had been defaced as he hung from the saddle stirrup while the mare ran.

This day and tomorrow, he thought as he raised himself to a sitting position in the bed, and the day after and the next day. And he was comforted a little by the thought. Even so great a thing as death happens in its moment of time and is sealed there. The living are borne from the instant of its occurrence. Each moment they are farther away. Flowing time bears them from the traps of contumely and the cesspools of sorrow and beyond all breached invulnerable walls.

He looked yet again at Danny, who was asleep or looking elsewhere so that his lids shadowed his eyes. He searched carefully the unguarded countenance, not aware of what he was seeking. But he found nothing, neither sign nor promise. So their relationship rested in equilibrium until it should be resumed in the full and active day. He rested a moment longer sitting on the bed as if gathering strength to make a supreme effort. As he sat thus remembering the events of the day before he felt the tightness within himself beginning to relax. He felt as if he had been tightly bound up with cloths and his father in dying had taken hold of the cloths and unwound them. He felt himself expanding outward until he filled the natural boundaries of his being. He felt easy and free within himself as the foot feels in a shoe that fits it.

He rose and clothed himself and then composing his face he went soberly down the stairs.

4

EZRA

The Idiot sprang from sleep and pivoted from under the covers, from the parenthesis of Danny's body, and stood poised a moment on the floor by the side of the bed. His face shone clear and beautiful in the early light; now inhabited by his waking eyes his face still bore the pure peace of sleep upon every feature. He stood a moment staring at Danny, smiling at him, his smile like the blessing of a saint pure in heart, and then he uttered his whole vocabulary, a series of three sounds, "Boodle, boodle, boodle!" which no one had ever been able to interpret. To the Preacher, when he had been alive, they had always suggested the handwriting on Belshazzar's wall: *mene, mene, tekel.* But to the old woman Mercidy they were terms of endearment, for she loved him with a fierce and protecting love, as if his simplicity made it necessary to erect the fort of her old bones between him and harm.

But he was invulnerable. He was like a wall without crevice to harbor the ruin of water from the rains and dews. He was like a bright steel ball sealed in glass. He was immune to the acids of life, the sorrows and trials and joys that rust and corrode the metal of man's being.

Invulnerable he stood by the side of the bed, in his shirttails, as he had been sleeping. A moment he stood, and then as Danny made a move to rise and force him into his pants he clapped his hands together and cried, "Boodle, boodle, boodle!" and bounded for the stairs.

The sound of weeping that came to him on waking prisoned in the vacuum of his brain and was without meaning. Below stairs was bread. The memory of the taste of bread was upon his tongue and his belly was empty from the famine of the night passed. He sped for the stairs, and Danny's hands upon his middle slipped from his bare hips across the soft, yielding flesh of his buttocks and came together against each other, with nothing but the feel of his flesh to close upon.

Down the stairs the Idiot ran, urged now by the hands that would detain him, (as well as his hunger), his shirttails flagging out behind him. In a moment he was on the floor below, through the rooms, running, his feet pattering on the bare floor and on his tongue the memory of the taste of bread.

When he entered the room where the people of the wake were gathered he looked about for the familiar faces, for his mother's or the old woman Mercidy's, but they were not there. He questioned the room with his whole vocabulary, "Boodle, boodle, boodle?" And for a moment the people looked at each other, covertly, as if someone in their midst had committed an indiscretion they were forced, out of courtesy, to overlook. The sea of faces, strange and without significance, swirled around him and then he saw the figure in the shroud and came and stood staring at it. He stood before the shrouded figure and clapped his hands together and cried, "Boodle, boodle, boodle!" His face, as he turned it to the people of the wake, was fresh and clear and beautiful, the pure peace of sleep still upon every feature.

Affronted, the people avoided him with their eyes, and Mercidy heard him from the room where she was with Mary and came and led him toward the kitchen. When he saw they were going to the kitchen he clapped his hands and cried out again.

"Boodle, boodle, boodle!" he sang out joyfully, upon his tongue the memory of the taste of bread.

5

MARY

Mary was already awake when the light began to invade the valley and send its salutation through the upstairs north window to waken Danny and the other three sleepers above stairs. While they lay remote in sleep's kingdom, inviolate except for the intrusion of dreams, she had not slept but oscillated between the dead sleeper in the largest room and the living sleeper, the child, in her own bedroom.

Over both she wept.

She wept over the one because he died and over the other because he lived. She saw in her grief how there was the same destination for both and a refrain began to run through her mind, like a phrase from an old song one hums without thinking of the words. Death's is the loneliest land. Not a leaf in death's kingdom, nor the wind nor the rain falling. The child was guilty. He had thrust like a wedge between the man, her husband, and life, and the thrust was greater than his hold on life and the child had won. The child was guilty. Nor the rain nor the wind in death's kingdom.

It seemed to her that she flowed as a stream between the two banks of life and death. When the current of herself was strongest toward the banks of death she flowed to her husband in the largest room. She would kneel by his side and weep until a woman of the wake would come and take her gently by the shoulders and say gently, "Sleep now, you will need your strength," and lead her to her own room.

In her own room Mercidy, the old woman, her mother-in-law, sat in a rocker and held the child that woke and slept as the very young do. The old woman held the child and rocked back and forth, its young life bundled safely in her frail old arms; and her face was as grave and gray as a stone in the field but it was not marked with tears. The old woman had no tears for death. She had care for life and the cradling of life in the arms of the dying. She was very old and she sat in the chair with the very young in her arms, the child like the child her son, lying dead in the largest room, had been. But she did not weep. It was as if she said to the dead: Wait a bit farther on, I will bring the child a little on the way, on the marvelous and terrible pilgrimage. To die is nothing, it is to enter the ark. The dead are safe forever. They have passed over to safety, their way is shut. Come, let us tremble for the safety of the living on the way.

The old woman seldom gave her eyes to Mary. When she did there was in them only sorrow for her sorrow and no condemnation, though it was she and not the child who was guilty. The child was proof of her guilt. The old woman suspected that she held in her arms the child of a stranger to her blood, yet she comforted it when it woke and held it when it slept.

Mary could not bear to see the child for long and then she would flow back to the sleeper in the shroud.

O death's is the loneliest land.

Nor a stone nor a leaf in death's kingdom.

She moved unseeing among the people of the wake who sat about the largest room and conversed among themselves but in undertones, as befitting those who sat at the side of the dead. Not that the dead may be disturbed by noise, though it should be loud enough to wake the living on the other side of the world. No. But since the first watchers sat by the first dead, paying the god of change from activity to stillness the tribute of half the volume of their voices, people have sat thus. They speak in undertones about their own affairs and about the affairs of the dead and the affairs of the bereaved, but they never raise their voices and they are never merry.

Mary wept by the side of her husband. It was not the loss of him that moved her to such sobs, but the thought of her husband's loss of himself. She had once loved him completely, but her husband was a strange man. He had once loved her completely also, but that was before he had tasted of the vials of righteousness that are sometimes poison to the whole man, withering him to half his normal stature. Since he had heard the Call to go preach he had demanded the love of her soul and fled from the love of her body. He did not know, or refused to admit, that she could not give him the one and withhold the other. And he was often forced by his own to accept the love of her body and employ it viciously. But afterward he hated himself, and her also, and went on long pilgrimages in the lean land of the spirit. He trembled behind the thin door of the spirit and ached to pass through to the warm sensual world beyond, but the specter of guilt stood at the door with an admonishing hand raised and he seldom dared ignore the warning.

And she could feel the force of his struggle but not sympathize with it. And now that the struggle was ended she felt no sorrow for her own loss, for it had been endured and was over. But he had lost himself also. Her he had lost long ago and now in what morass, in what wilderness had he lost himself? How utter was this loss of himself! How was the thin thread of the gold of life thinned to nothing in the uncleft darkness!

And she wept bitterly by his side.

Nor the rain nor the wind nor a stone in death's kingdom.

She came to her own room again and stood by the side of the old woman Mercidy and looked at the child in her arms and wept still. Her mother-in-law rose and gave her the child and said, "He is hungry, let him suckle." She took the child and sat in the chair while the old woman went into the other room. Through the open door she saw the old woman standing by the figure in the shroud. She stood there a long time and looked, but without a word or a sound of grief.

She was communing with her son and she did not know whether or not he felt what she was saying to him from the silence of her soul, but she had faith that he did and by faith is the thing accomplished.

She was saying to him:

O my son.

I set out in the morning before you and then we traveled together on the same road. Now you are gone on ahead. Wait. I am coming in God's good time.

For I was proud of you because you stood before the people. With the word of God in your mouth you stood before the people and told them of the way. We will go on together. Wait.

I remember how once we made a journey to a neighbor's house, and you were little and thought to run on ahead on the road. But you soon came to the end of your knowledge of the road, and you waited for me to come up with you and guide you on the journey, for I knew the way. When I came up to you where you rested on a stone you gave me the clouded look of the lost, you know you did not know the way further. But even so you did not return on the road to me. That was because you knew I would come to you. It is the same. If it is lonely on the way and the road is strange wait and we will go on together.

She heard the crying of the child from the other room and returned there and took him from his mother and comforted him to sleep again. And so doing she took leave of her son until she should find him waiting for her on the way.

But Mary returned to the largest room and stood by the shrouded figure and wept with renewed vigor, for the first light of morning was coming through the windows, and soon he would be placed in the best wagon of all those the people had brought to the wake, and carried to the cemetery and shut up, a tenant in the house of darkness forever. She wept for the wounding of the man who would never be healed. He was cleft in his spirit and now there was no more time to heal the cleavage. He went damaged into death and she loved wholeness and there was no more time for wholeness to be accomplished.

And suddenly she wept for herself.

Until this moment she had never admitted that death could come. For she had the confidence of the traveler in the middle of the journey that the journey would never end, and the confidence of the laborer at noon that the night would never come, and the confidence of the lover at the beginning of love that love would never die. And his death had negated all these confidences. She saw that she herself would come to this same pass and be no more. Oh!

Now the people of the wake let her weep unmolested for there was not much time left. The beginning of the last journey was at hand for the figure in the shroud.

Death's is the loneliest land.

ABNER

Abner came last into the house, heaving his ponderous weight from the barn where he had slept in the hayloft. When he woke it was not yet light. He was not certain where he was, though he must be in the hayloft because something was sticking him in the fat sides.

He had refused to sleep in his lean-to by the kitchen where he had slept since coming to the Preacher's house a dozen years before. He could not bear the sound of the crying women and the continual low thunder of movement within the house. When the first neighbors began to arrive for the wake he slipped from the house and made his way toward the barn in the falling night, muttering prayers and incantations he only half remembered.

When he woke he saw first the bulk of his own belly that rose before his eyes like a minor hill in the mountain range that ran west of the house. He was pleased with the sight of it, for he took his bulk as a great comfort and the best of insurance against the ills that seemed to beset people of lesser stature and weight. He had never been sick a day in his life and had never encountered a situation that fully tested the strength that dwelt in his mighty muscles. He was like a mountain on the loose. The first time the Preacher saw him laugh he was reminded of Isaiah's hills dancing together with glee. The Preacher had set great store by Abner, though he was slow in his mind, as if his great weight predominated there also.

Abner delayed his going to the house as long as possible. With the coming of light he rose and came down from the hayloft and fed the stock and scattered grain to the chir-

chir-chirrning hens and dallied with other small tasks as long as he was able. Yet the time came when he had to go into the house, out of respect for the Preacher. He entered by the kitchen and paused by the wash bench to wash his face and comb his graying hair, so that his appearance should bring no shame upon the man without his face in the largest room, the man who had stood his security by employing him for the past dozen years.

When he entered the largest room they were all there; and if he had not known them he could have told those of the fellowship of grief by their faces, he could have singled them out from those others, the comforters come to succor those of the fellowship of grief.

THE PREACHER

The other member of that household did not wake. The last thing he had been thinking was of a time long gone, passed away day by day like dollar bills counted and passed over one by one to another in payment of a debt. He had been thinking that the currency of days had been unequal to the debt he owed. He had not been able to settle the debt and find peace. Perhaps if he were allowed enough of the currency to pass across his palms . . . perhaps . . . but then the thing happened that scrambled his thoughts hopelessly. The mare plunged forward suddenly and he was thrown from the saddle. His foot turned in the left stirrup and caught there. He was dragged to death, flying by the mare's side, over the stony ground.

8

So all of that household were awake, except the one. None knew whether he woke or slept or was and would be no more; but all knew, except the Idiot who did not know to care, that if he woke it was not this side of mortality. There was that gulf between them across which they could not shout to bid him a good morning.

PART II

THE OUTWARD JOURNEY

I

There had been a time, the major portion of their lives, when Uncle Enid and Danny had not known the Preacher nor his family. The web of fate that drew them toward the Preacher's household looped them with its first strand on a January noon when they harnessed the mare to the wagon and set forth on a journey through a fall of snow.

Yet during the three days they were on the road there was nothing forewarning them that they approached the Preacher's house where, once arrived, their lives would never be the same again, until the morning of the third day when they stopped before a house they had never seen and offered a stranger a ride in their wagon.

The two of them were leaving the house where they had been born, a generation apart, and the reason for their departure was unclear, even to the man who felt it only as a nebulous desire clouding his life; he wished to leave the farm that demanded more loyalties than a wife and adventure into the great world of which he had heard good report from his friends who returned from beyond the somnolent horizons of his pocket of earth.

When the opportunity came he sold the farm to his neighbor, and on a January noon he and the boy climbed into the wagon and set their faces outward toward the unknown. They left security behind them, exchanging it for adventurous chancing into the world beyond the borders of their own county.

It began to snow on the hour of their setting forth.

2

UNCLE ENID

From time to time as he drove Uncle Enid rested his fore-arm against the money belt he had made from a sugar sack and strings and tied about his middle before setting out. The belt contained all the money he had got for the farm and the animals and the house plunder. It was a sizable sum, con-taining, besides, all he had saved through years of frugal living. The weight of the money pulled against his flesh and he could see in his mind the nest of greenbacks and the cluster of silver pieces in the bag. The money represented his free-dom from the small and great tyrannies of life on the farm and the fine bulk of it resting in safety against his body set up a pleasurable feeling that tingled in his nerve ends.

Yet a gold piece that had been his particular treasure was missing from the hoard. He remembered clearly his sharp sense of loss when he first discovered it was gone from among the pieces of money. When he thought of the gold piece there was an emptiness in him like that of hunger. He went back in his mind now to the day, shortly after he had sold the farm to Tully, when he went to the crock that served him as a bank to reassure himself of his great fortune:

The money was all there except the gold piece. Its glow was absent from the flash of the silver and the dull-green shining of the bills. He was stunned. He let the silver pour through his fingers again but the gold piece did not reap-pear among the silver coins, as he knew it would not though he could not accept the fact that it was missing from the nest of coins. He crushed the bills in his hands, thinking if the gold piece was invisible among their folds he would feel its

golden bulk resisting the pressure of his fingers. He did feel
the curving edge of a coin as his fingers tightened on the bills
and he was dizzy with relief, but when he had straightened
the bills out one by one to come on the coin he found it to be
yet another coin of silver. For a moment he hated the silver
coin because it was not the gold piece.

"It's gone," he said to himself. He stood looking at the pile
of money that bulked on the cupboard shelf, opening and
closing his fingers as he regarded it. He seemed to be waiting
for the silver coins and the green bills to say where the gold
piece had gone from among them. He looked at them a long
time. Then he put the money in the crock again and stuffed
the old gingham rag in the top and replaced it on the cupboard
shelf.

"Gone," he said to himself, turning from the crock and the
cupboard toward the door through which a shaft of winter
sunlight as gold as the lost coin was pouring. He made as if to
go out the door, then turned back to the cupboard and removed the crock and searched carefully the shelf on which
the crock rested. The coin was not there.

"Somebody stole it," he said. He pulled the gingham rag
from the crock and shook it carefully, but nothing fell from
its folds. Only a little dust went up, golden in color, dullish
golden.

Then he began to count the money feverishly. He made the
silver pieces clink against each other in a fury of clinking. He
had only been admiring the money when he discovered the
gold piece missing. For moments after the discovery he had
hoped that it was only misplaced, had fallen on the shelf or
by some chance got entangled in the old rag that served both
to stop the top of the crock and disguise its contents. But
someone must have taken the gold piece, and if so, how much
more besides? The coins rattled against each other in his

haste of counting. The bills slap-slap-slapped against each other as he ran up their total in his mind.

Nothing was missing but the gold piece.

It was damned queer.

He selected a dollar at random from the silver and stood throwing it into the air and catching it as it came down. He took particular pains to make it reverse itself in the air with each throw, yet his mind was not on the silver dollar. His mind had gone in search of the gold piece.

There had been but the one gold piece in all the money.

It had shone like the moon when the air is smoky at its rising.

He began to follow it from the beginning in his mind in hopes of tracing it down, even to the place where it must now be, eluding him.

He was crouching on the ground, on his heels, with his neighbor Tully facing him. They had concluded the interminable palaver that is the ritual of the country tradesman and agreed upon terms for the transference of the farm from his possession to Tully's.

"Three hundred in greenbacks," Tully said, counting it out on his knee in fives, tens, and ones.

"Twenty-five in silver," Tully had the silver in a little bag tied with a drawstring. He poured the contents of the bag on the ground and stacked it in piles, each coin after its kind, dime upon dime, quarter upon quarter, half dollar upon half dollar and silver dollars after their kind. Their bright milled edges glittered in the sun.

There was a pause, and Uncle Enid looked at Tully expectantly while he rested on his heels, his hands hanging slack between his open knees, not yet rising to go exploring his pocket for the remaining money. After a moment Tully raised his hand to the pocket on the bib of his overalls and reached into it with stubby forefinger and slowly brought forth the gold piece from the pocket's depth. It emerged from between the denim-blue lips of the pocket like the sun emerging from between two thunderheads.

That was the first he had seen of the gold piece.

Tully held the coin in the palm of his cupped hand and his eyes dwelt on it fondly. He, too, looked at the coin, admiring its clean stamp and the fine shine of its alloy. He suddenly wanted the coin very much. In all his life he had never possessed a gold piece.

"I meant to keep the gold piece," Tully said. "If I could have raised the money without throwing in the gold piece . . ." he held it still in his hand, turning it from side to side. "Got it a long time ago in a trade with Old Harkins. Dead now. You remember Old Harkins?"

He remembered and nodded. His own palm tingled with desire to feel the weight of the gold piece.

"Kept it for a good-luck piece," Tully went on. "Never spent it, hard up a lot of times but never did spend the gold piece."

Uncle Enid nodded again, keeping his eyes on the gold piece. He might hang it from his watch chain.

"No sense being foolish about a piece of money, though," Tully said. He stretched out his hand, slowly, reluctantly, and transferred the gold piece from his own palm to Uncle Enid's. "Did mean to keep it," he said, "but it spends as good as greenback."

"Twenty in gold."

And so the deal by which Tully came into possession of his farm was completed.

"Well," he had said, "you've got yourself a fine farm. With the land you've bought added to what you had already nobody in the county's got a better."

Tully, pleased, nodded his head three times and the thought of the land he now owned returned a greater shining to his eyes than the surrender of the gold piece had taken away.

He left Tully then, and on the way to the farm that had been his own his heart sank to think that the ancestral acres that had underwritten the security of his forefathers for generations were no longer his. But the weight of the silver and the bulk of the greenbacks reassured him; and nestled in his watch pocket was the twenty-dollar gold piece. Finally it came in his mind to represent the freedom he had bought with the sale of the farm. A man has a right to a while of freedom before he dies, he thought. As long as a man is young and able security can dwell in his muscles as well as in property. Inside himself he felt the strength of his body, firm and supple as a hickory sapling, and his fear disappeared. He carried his freedom, minted in a mint, printed on a press, along the country road and when he reached the house where he was born he stored it in the old crock he had used to bank his extra change. He placed the coins and the bills in the crock and stuffed an old gingham rag into its throat and placed the crock where it had always rested on the top shelf of the kitchen cupboard.

All except the gold piece.

He kept the gold piece in his watch pocket. He had not yet decided what to do with it. Besides, he wanted it on his person so he could hold it in his hand from time to time.

That was how he had come into possession of the gold piece, and now it was gone.

He stood, still with the silver dollar in his hand, and went back in his mind to take up the history of the gold piece.

It was too much money to hang on a watch chain. If it had been a two-dollar-and-a-half piece or even a five-dollar one it would have made a fine charm to hang at the chain's end.

But not a twenty-dollar piece. It would be putting on airs. Yet he held the coin to the end of the chain to try it how it would look, and all his dark ancestors came from the cells of his body and the fields of his flesh and looked at him and said, "Ha!" He was almost as outraged as they by the look of a twenty-dollar gold piece at his chain's end, and he put the coin in his pocket again and the scorn left the faces of his dark ancestors and they faded away.

Instead of a charm for his watch chain he would keep it as a shield against the worm of want, should the strength that dwelt in his body fail for a time. And it was big enough to hide Danny, to enfold him for a long time against hunger, and it had the power to hire his healing if he should become ill. He had a momentary vision of Danny in that golden robe, his fine face shining with a goldish cast through the gold of the coin encompassing him.

So he gave up the idea of hanging the coin from his watch chain, but he carried it in his watch pocket as he went about his work, the tasks life on the farm demanded doing in the old age of the year. He gathered corn and stored roughage in the cavernous barn loft with a peculiar zest, thinking: The last time, the last time. On leaving the farm he meant to work at a sawmill or go to the smelters at the copper works not far away and work there.

He often took the coin from his pocket when Danny was not with him to see the action and looked at it and admired it. He took the coin as gold and round as the day and held it in his hand and let the two medallions, the day and the coin, flash fire from each other. It became dearer each day and finally it came to represent all the money, itself, the silver and the greenbacks safe in the glazed crock.

After he had carried the coin for a month he lost it.

A certain night he took his watch from his pocket to wind

it. As he was winding the watch he noticed there were fine scratches on the watch crystal. The coin, he concluded, was scratching the face of the watch. He must think of a way to keep them separated in his pocket. Wrap the coin in a piece of cloth perhaps. He probed into the pocket with his forefinger, reaching for the coin.

It was not there.

He sat down, filled with dismay.

The gold piece would be difficult to find. He had had it at noon that day. At noon he had taken it from his pocket and rested himself by looking at it. When he looked at the coin the tiredness flowed out of his muscles like the water from a pool when its dam is broken. That day he had finished hauling the corn from the south bottom. He could have lost it in the field. He could have lost it in the wagon bed, stooping over it to throw the corn from the bed into the crib. It could have lodged in the husk of an ear of corn and traveled with it into the crib. If so he would never find it.

His dismay deepened. He rose as if to go in search of the coin. The night was too dark. There was no use going in search of the bright coin in that unbroken darkness. Even so gold a coin could not penetrate the night and announce itself by dazzles of golden light. He must wait for day.

He was up before the sun and said he must go out and Danny stood watching him intently as he went from the house, searching the ground in the frosty light of early morning for the coin. He retraced the wagon tracks along the road to the south bottom, walking slowly, examining the tracks with undivided attention. Once he looked ahead and saw a shining in the right wagon track a few yards ahead. It sent shafts of light from the sun into the absorbing air. His heart lifted and he hurried toward the object.

It was a piece of mica set in a pebble of sandstone that glittered in the sun.

He did not find it in the field, nor in the wagon bed, nor about the crib.

"Tully begrudged me the gold piece," he said at the end of the first day of the Days of the Lost Gold Piece. In the days that followed he went about his work as usual but his eyes were always searching for the missing coin; even where he had not been on the day of loss he sought it.

One night he took the crock from the shelf and looked into it. "If I had put the gold piece with the other money," he said, and replaced the crock.

Then on a morning he took his pail and went to the feed room of the barn for morning feed for the cow. The room was littered with straws and slivers of shucks, and when he moved a golden dust rose up from his feet into the block of sunlight that prisoned in the door. As he stooped to put the meal in the feed pail he saw the coin.

It was lying in the straw litter.

It had fallen from his pocket earlier as he bent above the feed pail. He scooped it up with a short cry of joy. The hand that retrieved the gold piece trembled, and the trembling increased the glittering of the gold piece as it rested in his hand in the glow of the morning sun.

That was the first time he had lost it but not the last by two.

He had returned the gold piece to his pocket wrapped in a fold of his linen handkerchief. He returned it with a sense of thankfulness and because its bulk was increased by the wrapping he had only to put his hand against the pocket to know it was there, safe in his bosom like the salvation of the Lord prisoned in the bosom of saints.

The days wheeled one after the other like great golden

coins in the weeks following, the Days of the Found Gold Piece. The days were like his coin except their reverse sides showed obsidian, like the stone of the arrows left in his fields by the Indians, themselves shot by the bowstring of time beyond the land of their nativity. He was busy with gathering the harvest into the barn, to the last ear of corn, to the last golden pumpkin, to the last bronze bundle of fodder. His kitchen walls were strung with dried beans and slender scarlet peppers that hung like beads about the slender necks of nails driven into the wall to hold them. He paused at times to wonder who would reap the benefits of his careful husbandry of the autumn harvest, since he could not carry in his faring a tithe of all he had gathered.

When he saw Tully infrequently he observed about him the airs of an owner of extensive property. He did not resent these airs, though in the days before he had sold him the farm Tully and he met as equals, their relationship long established on the basis of ownership of equal possessions. These airs that Tully now gave himself were the reward of long skimping in order to save enough money to buy Uncle Enid's property.

"If I could take possession right away," Tully would say, "I could get some plowing done before spring. It's going to push me to get all the land in, now there are so many acres to plow."

"Most any time now," he would say, keeping in mind the terms of their agreement whereby he could not be evicted before the New Year, but seeming to wish to oblige Tully. "Got to have a sale and be rid of the corn and plunder."

"I need to extend the ditch in the south bottom," Tully would say. "Ground's a little sobby beyond the head of the ditch. If I could take over right away...."

"Right at once now," he would answer.

So he was busy as the days of late autumn wheeled into

winter. He thought of the gold piece less often, and in the press of several busy days not at all.

He was catching water from the trough when his eyes fell upon something at the edge of the pond. It was vaguely familiar, it moved something in his mind but he stood preoccupied with the song of the water from the trough against the sides of the bucket, a tune running from treble to bass as the level of the water rose. As he took the bucket from the trough his eyes brushed the scrap at the pond's edge and something electric swept through him. He set the bucket down, spilling the water, and took up the linen scrap from the pond. He unfolded the cloth to the gold piece within, and the film of wetness added to the sheen of its luster.

He did not know when he had lost it, but he went to the crock and placed the gold piece in the nest of greenbacks with the silver pieces. Its golden shine warred with the flashing of the silver coins.

Thereafter he went without fear of the coin slipping from his pocket.

So he followed the gold piece in his mind to the time when it was deposited in the crock. He yearned to see beyond the crock then to the coin itself, wherever it was. But he had followed it in vain in his mind. He found no clue that would be helpful in locating the gold piece. His vision of it, lying lost and golden in a cleft of darkness, faded to nothing.

It could not have been lost from the crock.

Someone had taken it.

He skirted the possible thief in his mind. He felt suddenly tired as he stood looking into the crock. As he made a motion toward the crock a cloud came over the sun.

The gold was even gone out of the day.

He made to lift the crock and replace it in its usual position on the top cupboard shelf. Then for the first time he was aware of the silver dollar in his hand. He removed the gingham rag and flung the coin angrily into the crock. It rang against the glazed sides of the crock and came to rest with a final dull clank among the other coins. He took the crock into his hands then, but instead of placing it on the cupboard shelf he turned abruptly to his own room. There he placed the crock on a shelf of the clothes press and pulled his shirts over it. They hid the crock in a random fold of their disarray.

"I coveted it too much. The Lord wouldn't let me keep it," he said, taking leave of the gold piece. He turned then and went through the door looking for Danny. He had it in his mind to leave the farm as soon as possible.

When the time of their going forth arrived, as the first preparation for the journey he took the money less the gold piece and placed it in the bag he had made for it, and tied it about his middle. Now he rode in the wagon through the falling snow and the loss of the gold piece was in his mind, and he could think of nothing to do with the loss except endure it to dullness and at length to dust.

3

DANNY

To remember, Danny thought.

He had been preoccupied with the promise in the sky when Uncle Enid came that day from visiting the crock and passed like a wraith through the field of his vision. Clouds fluffy and soft as sheep's wool scudded before the wind from the sky's northwest corner. A tentative snowdrop fell now and then from the racing clouds. These represented partial payment of a note the sky had signed on a blustery day early in October, when a few flakes, the first of the year, fell to disappear as soon as fallen.

It was his hope that now the sky meant to pay the note in full, and yet the hope ran counter to his weather wisdom. The clouds were rough and jumbled like a field of boulders, and he had come to expect a respectable snow only from a sky cloud as smooth as glass, gray and unmoving. The turbulence of the air was a factor against the fulfillment of his hope also, for snow wants stillness to fall through. Should his hope prevail over the natural obstacles to its fulfillment he was prepared to pay the sky a full measure of delight.

Later through his speculation the voice of Uncle Enid came up from the barn, calling his name. He stood at the woodpile under the larger of two golden maples that stood at the flank of the house like guards posted to hold it from surprise attack from the elements, hearing the voice that came to him soft and rounded by its passage through the space from the barn to the house. He did not respond to the call. I am here already, he thought, and he filed the call away in the part of his brain reserved for unfinished matters and carried an armful of wood from the woodpile to the back porch. Ordinarily the business of getting wood for the night was a dull chore but the promise of snow made it exciting, lifted it into the realm of important matters, as if he laid in food against a siege.

His uncle's voice came to him again, rounded and modulated by its thrust through the space from his uncle to himself, and he listened carefully, but this time his uncle was not calling his name. He was calling the hogs in the lot for their afternoon feed. Having gone to the barn on other matters and not being able to fulfill them his uncle nevertheless refused to waste the energy that had carried him there, and so he was feeding the hogs and no doubt would feed the other animals their evening feed before returning to the house in the quest of himself, Danny.

This switch of attention on his uncle's part freed him for moments from the constraint of his authority. But the purity of his release from his uncle was colored with speculation concerning his want with him at all.

For punishment?

For reward?

Through the exercise of these two powers his uncle validated their relationship as father and son, though they were not father and son, but the fact that both seemed to him now beyond the periphery of likelihood left him to fruitless speculation that itched like a rash in his mind. He made a small mountain of wood rise on the back porch, then in the silence that came up from the barn like a tide in the wake of his uncle's voice he went into the kitchen by way of the hall that ran from the back to the front porch, dividing the short end of the L-shaped structure from the long end that served as the living quarters of the house. On his way through the hall he passed the door of his own room and had a momentary vision of himself lying in his bed asleep. He looked at the mirror features of his face a moment before the vision was lost in a switch of interest. He passed Uncle Enid's room on the other side of the hall exactly opposite his own, and the two Nobody's Rooms lying on either side of the hall, dark foreboding domains of mystery.

When he entered the kitchen he looked first at the cupboard, and it assumed its familiar image in his mind, yet it was not exactly the same. He stood regarding the cupboard while the hunger that had brought him to the kitchen subsided and was forgotten in the effort to determine what made the cupboard strange in its familiarity. Suddenly his mind restored the object missing from the image of the cupboard.

The crock that flowered with an old gingham rag was gone.

When he discovered this a tendril of an emotion he did not understand began to grow in his mind. He turned his head from where he stood and looked through the door, and because his uncle was not on the path a feeling of relief swept through him like a gust of wind. He took a piece of sweetbread from the second shelf of the cupboard and went through the hall nibbling at it.

Something of stealth came over him then; there was a dread of his uncle on his spirit. In a pause he made to listen he heard that silence still flowed from the barn. Then he heard his uncle wading in the silence and, urged away from him, he stepped from the porch on the side of the house opposite the path side. He went toward the barn as his uncle came from there. They moved in opposite directions, the house between them.

And Danny was first aware then that between them was the lost and the taken, the gold piece.

On the path to the barn he heard his uncle call him again, his voice rising loud and urgent from the doorway of the house. He tried to ignore the call altogether but it remained, a cord binding their two entities that were otherwise planetary in their separate orbits of action.

With the cord of his uncle's voice binding them he went to the barn.

Besides his Uncle Enid, who was at its center, his world was populated by these others: Bessie the cow, the bull who was known as Blackie, the mare, without name since she was not a primary character, and Five-Pigs the sow and her current offspring. With the exception of the latter these lived in the nether regions of the barn, in the stables that were dark and stuffy under the huge loft that smelled of fodder and hay.

He paused at the hog lot where Five-Pigs was eating the corn his uncle had fed her. She placed a large divided foot on the ears and bit the grains from the cobs. As he leaned over the fence the sow grunted in recognition, and he climbed the fence and stood among the pigs that were too young to eat the corn. They tugged at their mother's side, and he pulled them away and offered them the remainder of his sweetbread. They smelled of it and made tentative efforts to take it into their mouths, then returned to the wrinkled dugs of their mother. He stooped and tickled a pig on its pink belly and it leaned against his hand, leaning harder and harder until he removed his hand and the pig lay for a moment on its side on the ground.

"Old Five-Pigs," he said to the sow. There was logic in the name because for some reason she always gave birth to five pigs. She was large and shaggy, a sandstone color; her ears hung before her face hiding her little eyes that looked out small and mean from between straggly eyebrows. The expression of her eyes belied her nature for she was friendly and gentle and bore with his pranking with as much grace as an old woman shows to the idle and foolish pranking of the young.

"Old Five-Pigs," he said again and laid his hand on her

leathery back, folding his fingers into her rough hair. The sow replied with a grunt and a flipping of her crusty tail.

At that moment his uncle called him yet again and his voice had grown sharp. He made the gesture of Not Coming which consisted of an impatient screwing up of his face and entered the barn. The hallway was littered with straw and fodder shatters and numberless worn plows and broken pieces of iron saved for emergencies of mending that never occurred stuck from cracks in the wall. He went through the tunnel of hallway, looking first toward the house. His uncle was nowhere in sight and he climbed then into the loft and threw down three bronze bundles of fodder.

These he gave to the forage-eating animals that lived in the barn. One to Bessie, so named because his uncle had bought her from a woman of the neighborhood named Bessie Teague. Bessie was a claybank with a dull-white star in her forehead. She did not converse with him in her language, as the sow did, but she had eloquent eyes. As he threw the bundle of fodder into her stall she looked at him with a clear grateful stare. He closed the door upon her and as he did so it occurred to him suddenly that her udder was like a pot in which his uncle did their washings by the brook's side.

The second bundle of fodder he gave to the bull. He had discovered Blackie two years before by an elder clump in the pasture where he had been birthed by Bessie. He was totally black except for a smudge of white that stained the purity of his color near his right flank. Blackie was playful like himself and though he had been warned that the bull might hurt him he disregarded the warning. When the bull was turned to pasture they would play together, feinting toward each other, butting their heads together lightly in a pantomime of fight.

He fed the third bundle of fodder to the mare, not lingering at the door of her stall because of all the animals she was most a stranger. Not that there was any evil in her, she was almost as placid as the cow, yet because she contained great potentials of strength and speed he was afraid of her.

After the mare there was nothing more to feed, and he went from the hallway into the light of the enormous round day. The barnyard fowls converged around him as he came from the barn but he paid no attention to them. He had never been able to establish any sort of contact with the fowls, as he had with the other inhabitants of the farmstead. Because of this lack of understanding between them he even disliked the fowls, especially the speckled guineas that scattered to the woods when disturbed and cried pot-rack-pot-rack-pot-rack for hours with ear-shattering shrillness.

He was already on his way to the house when his uncle called him again, shouting, the irritation that was beginning to grow in him riding the waves of his voice. He had entirely lost the trace of the strange emotion that stirred him as he beheld the absence of the crock. His spirit was warmed and lifted through contact with the animals. The image of the coin guilt had minted in his mind had melted and run down into the slag of his subconscious.

"Danny!" his uncle shouted from the kitchen door. He smiled faintly and then put on the empty face with which he confronted his uncle when in doubt of his reception. It began to snow again in great erratic drops and he removed the nothing from his face and let delight shine there for a moment. The snow touched him with a chaste cool touch and as he ran along the path he clapped his hands together and sang out, "The Old Woman in the sky is picking her geese!"

Now in the wagon the gold piece was between them again. It rested now in the purse his uncle had given to encourage him in thrift. It rested there with the three pennies that had comprised his whole fortune before he had taken the gold piece. He did not know the value of the gold piece. He had taken it because it was beautiful.

He wished the gold piece back in the crock and its taking washed from his mind and removed from between him and his uncle, who drove the mare through the falling snow withdrawn and partially lost to him by the act that defiled and punished him, and was all the more regrettable because it was as irrevocable as the hour in which he stole.

4

The gold piece had not been between them as they sat at the long kitchen table, on the eve of the promising sky, eating by lamplight. They sat at the table in the house that did not know the touch of women eating from an excessively clean table covered with green oilcloth. The small brass lamp rested in the center of the table, in an island of darkness that was the shadow of its base. Uncle Enid sat on the side next the stove in order to be handy to it and Danny faced him from the opposite side of the table. They never ate side by side for if they had they would have been unable to see each other without a craning and bending of necks and part of the communication between them would have been lost.

He says things without speaking, Danny thought. I finger about in my plate and his face darkens because I am supposed to use my fork and not my fingers. He doesn't say anything but I look at his darkened face and it makes me uncomfortable. I pick up my fork and use it to corner the fat back in the peas on my plate and his face lightens and we are together again. His own face darkened and lightened like fields when clouds are many but broken and sweep intermittently between the earth and sun.

They talked little in words at meals for there was nothing much to talk about and through the years that they had lived together they had come to understand each other's gestures and facial expressions and words were unnecessary between them.

Yet Danny had stumbled on a new discovery in the act of listening to his uncle call him from the barn earlier in the afternoon. He had been aware for some time of the possibility of the thing he had discovered, but it burst upon him suddenly like all discoveries do and it excited him greatly.

"I know what color talking is," he said as he helped himself to a plate of black-eyed peas.

"What color, then?" Uncle Enid said. It was a trait of his that he never showed surprise. If someone had announced, as to the fowls in the fairy story, that the sky was falling he would have turned without haste to look and see for himself.

"It's black," Danny said. "When you say, bring a bucket of water, the words sound black."

Uncle Enid smiled and looked at him with amusement growing in his eyes.

"When you yell," Danny said, "it sounds red."

"It does, does it?" Uncle Enid said.

"Except not exactly," Danny said. "It sounds like red and yellow mixed."

"What color does a baby cry?" Uncle Enid said.

"Why, it cries about the same color of a rock," Danny said. He was afraid that his uncle was beginning to make fun of him. The light of amusement grew in his eyes. It danced there like a swarm of midges early in the morning.

"Rocks are all colors," Uncle Enid said.

"It cries the color of a flint rock," Danny said.

"Gray or white or yellow?" Uncle Enid said.

"Gray," Danny said, taking his choice of the colors of flint.

He was not anxious to continue the description of the colors of sound. He wanted more time to listen and determine the colors the sounding world made.

They sat in silence for a long while after they had finished eating. Danny began to droop with sleepiness. He made rings in the leavings in his plate with a slender forefinger and the figures he made ran together and then separated, closed and exploded as his consciousness wavered in the nelson bend of sleep.

After a while Uncle Enid lifted him and warmed him before the fire as he would an inanimate bundle. Then he carried him through the hall to his room and turned back the covers.

"I don't want to go to bed," Danny said on his way through the dark hall.

"Time," Uncle Enid said.

"It's too cold," Danny said.

"It's not much cold," Uncle Enid said, but he could tell from the way the wind struck the corner of the house that it had veered from southwest to north. It whistled in a lamenting cold voice about the eaves.

"Will it snow?" Danny said.

"Not while the wind's from the north," Uncle Enid said.

"I want it to snow," Danny said.

"All boys want it to snow," Uncle Enid said.

He lifted Danny and held him under the arms while he unbuttoned his overalls and let them slip from his body to the floor. "I've got to quit this foolishness of putting you to bed," he said.

"I can get in bed," Danny said. But he stood on the sheepskin before his bed and made no move to crawl between the covers.

Uncle Enid lifted him and placed him in bed, then he tucked the covers around him to keep out the cold. He stood with the brass lamp in his hand and looked at Danny in silence. Danny regarded him in turn with a light quizzical stare.

"You forgot something," Uncle Enid said.

Danny closed his eyes and said swiftly in a subdued voice:

> "Now I lay me down to sleep
> I pray the Lord the watch to keep.
> If I should die before I wake
> I pray the Lord my soul to take.
> God bless Uncle Enid and God bless me."

Uncle Enid sighed. He meant to tell Danny that tomorrow he would go and arrange the sale and when they were rid of the goods they would go and try their luck in the wide world. Instead he turned to leave the room.

"Night," he said.

"Night," Danny said, and one listening could not have told whether they were commenting on the time of day or taking leave of each other for the solitary journey across the continent of sleep.

When Uncle Enid left him in the darkness Bessie and the sow and the pigs and Blackie and the mare passed like specters through his mind and he asked that they be blessed along with Uncle Enid and himself. Then from a sense of justice he summoned the fowls also. From this spectral procession a guinea took disturbed flight but its progress dissolved into nothingness and a wail of the north wind was sliced clean from its source by sleep which is a knife and nothing.

5

UNCLE ENID

Nor was the gold piece between them the following morning when the day of their faring was closer by one. Uncle Enid rose in the half-light of dawn, shivering in the cold air, the flesh of his legs pimpling where they were bare below his shirt. He stood on the outer rims of his feet, his insteps drawn away from the icy floor, hesitating to draw on his overalls. They were slick with cold as if with filth. The cold flowing about him urged him at last and he put first one leg through a hollow of cloth and then the other. He felt as if he were encased in ice. He stood trembling, trying to contract his flesh to bring it away from contact with the cold cloth. When the warmth of his flesh had communicated itself to the cloth he bent to ease his feet into his shoes, iron from the cold. When he made the first steps in them they would not bend.

When he stepped onto the porch for wood to build a fire the wind caught him, a wind so cold it felt wet to the skin. He hastened a backstick from the pile and overlaid the andirons with small sticks and lit the fire with rich pine knots he had gathered from fallen trees on the mountains. While he was outside getting wood for the fire he saw that a powder of snow lay on the low matted grass of the fields. There was snow as light as frost on the woodpile under the maples and the straw pile by the barn smoked in the chilly fire of snow.

When the fire roared at last, he sat with his hands folded over the end of the fire shovel, resting his head on his hands. He spread his legs wide to the heat, and as the warmth began to collect in his clothing he suddenly brought his knees together to shut it out. He was troubled and a little outraged at the suggestiveness the warm cloth imparted to his body where it bound against his crotch.

He rose and turned to build a fire in the stove.

He made biscuits and put them in a pan and took sausage from a mason jar where they were buried in a fog of grease and put them in another, setting the pan toward the back of the stove where the heat was less. When he was finished with his morning chores the food would be cooked. Though he was not now pressed for time he persisted in following the patterns of his habits. In the times of great activity on the farm his method of cooking gained him precious minutes in the fields.

In all his years he had never cooked a meal without feeling slightly outraged at performing what he considered a woman's task. It was his only ability developed to a high state of perfection of which he was not proud. He did not boast of his ability to cook among men as he did his ability to cradle wheat. His proficiency at cooking displeased him, as if it impugned his masculinity.

Thinking then of his desire to surrender his distaff duties brought inexplicably the sensation he had experienced before the fire.

While the food cooked on the stove he went to the barn and fed the animals. He stood at the opened doors of the stalls, observing with wonder the great gouts of breath the animals sent vivid into the cold morning air. In the vapor of their breathing that dissolved, not from edge to center but all at once, he saw suddenly a metaphor for the dispersal of life into the wide air of death.

On his way through the house again he called Danny and told him it was time to rise. He stood before his door, listening. There was no sound of activity within, and he went into the kitchen and set the table and placed the food upon it. Then he entered Danny's room and turned the covers from him. As the air struck his body Danny turned immediately from the pose of sleep and rose and clung to him for warmth until he held him away at arm's length and slapped him smartly on the buttocks and helped him into his overalls.

Going to the kitchen Danny saw that the niggard sky had failed to fulfill its promise.

"I wanted it to snow," he said.

"It didn't oblige you," Uncle Enid said in a bantering tone but his nephew looked at him with an affronted stare and he knew that he was very disappointed. Then he remembered with a dim sense of hurt because it came no more the sense of joy with which he had awakened to a morning of snow in the days of his boyhood.

"I guess snow's a boy's weather, all right," he said. Then he continued, "There isn't any snow but it's a special day still."

"What kind of a special day?" Danny said.

"I'll go and arrange a sale and when we are rid of the house plunder we will go away. We will go where there are things to do and people to see every day." He spoke in the spell of his own dreaming. It was later that he remembered the look his nephew flashed him, and so he was never able to determine whether it spoke of anxiety or disbelief.

6

UNCLE ENID

Neither could he say when he had come to accept the fact that Danny had taken the gold piece. Now with the house behind them and becoming already the property of memory he thought of the gold piece again and he was certain that Danny had taken it. I could say to him let me have the gold piece, he thought, and he would give it to me. But what would I say then? Then I would have proof that he had taken it and I would have to punish him yet not much for if I hurt him I hurt myself

If I never mention it

If I never

He will not say here it is and shrink from me and hurt me Because he is hurt.

Yet in stealing the coin Danny had also stolen of his love for him. The sum of the money was less and his love was less, even by the smallest degree, and the restoring of the first would not restore the second. Nothing would restore it.

Nothing will restore the taken away, he thought. And he thought of all he had ever lost, the little and the much, and though for some he had been recompensed the lost had never been returned.

Behold what has gone through a door.

Behold what has slipped from the hand.

He turned his mind then from loss and the gold piece and began to think about the days that led to their departure.

7

On the day of the sale a great clatter grew out of the morning silence. People of the neighborhood were arriving in wagons, on horses, in buggies; and others came afoot or pushing wheelbarrows to carry away their possible purchases. The women chattered like magpies while they poked about, disparaging the objects they especially wanted and had it in mind to buy. They found holes in the sheets where there were none. They argued the pots and pans were scoured to thinness. They shook the bedsteads until they clattered and said they were loose to the point of collapse.

The men said the corn was chaffy though it was firm and well filled. They said the fodder had been damaged in curing though it was as bright as morning, that the hay was full of dock. They milled and bargained and disputed among themselves about the value of this and that. They spread dinner on the ground and made a social of the day and when the meal was finished returned to their bargaining.

Tully bought the livestock, except the mare which would carry them on their faring, and said he would leave the animals in the barn seeing it was his own now.

Finally the people were all gone, each carrying the reluctant purchase with which he was well pleased. And Uncle Enid and Danny stood in the stripped house and looked at the small pile of belongings they had saved for the faring forth, the bedding for the journey that would serve for a pallet on the floor until they set out, the few utensils for cooking their meals over an open fire, their bundled clothes, and were strangers in the house they had known always.

In the afternoon Uncle Enid went and groomed the mare, and fed her additional rations because she was his one remaining animal.

8

New Year's morning Tully arrived with the first wagon-load of his house plunder and began to unload it in the yard. Uncle Enid came from the house and stood staring at him.

"I have the right," Tully said and indeed he did for they had agreed that the two of them might stay on in the house until the first of the year and then he and Danny must be gone from there.

"I can't get out today," Uncle Enid said, "It's going to snow."

Tully cocked a weather eye at the ceiling of clouds and agreed.

"You can stay with us," Tully said. "You can go when you like." And he drove away after a second load of his furnishings.

It was unthinkable to Uncle Enid to dwell for even one night as a guest in the house that had been his own. Besides, should it snow as he had prophesied, the date of their departure might be indefinitely delayed. They would go forth, looking to strangers for lodging, as they would have to do in any case until they were settled elsewhere. So when Tully arrived with his last load of furnishings, accompanied this time by his brood of towheads who stood about staring, he had his own wagon packed for the journey and the mare stood in her immemorial pose of patience between the wagon shafts. Even when it began to snow she stood impassive in her harness, without movement except for a flicker that ran through her skin now and then, clearing it of the falling flakes.

9

DANNY

Many had been the days of preparation and waiting, and these were filled with activity that tired their muscles and sent them exhausted to bed. Though they were not ordinary days they yet lacked the quality of the Day itself. The Day of the going forth.

Danny remembered it:

From his seat on the narrow board that spanned the wagon bed he watched his uncle as he investigated the harness before taking his own place in the wagon. When he was settled Uncle Enid spoke to the mare and she moved forward from the yard and into the road that led outward.

"Where are we going?" Danny said when they were upon the road.

His uncle was silent for a moment, thinking: Going forth. Like Columbus in the largest of his three small ships, the level sun breaking on the gentle waves before the wallowing prows. Like De Soto in his suit of iron, his horse's head pointing in the direction of the fabled cities. Like Boone in his coonskin cap, eyes peeled for Indians on the trail to the west. Going forth, the two of us, toward the next hill, the next country, the next state.

"Going away," he said finally.

As they drew farther and farther from it Danny looked back at the house that was half hidden by its guard of maples standing veined against the January sky. He shifted his gaze to the barn where Uncle Enid had kept the livestock before he sold the place to Tully, and he thought he saw Bessie disappear into the hallway. He could not be sure. The growing distance crept like blindness over his sight.

"What are you looking at?" Uncle Enid said.

Danny swung his gaze to his uncle's face. It wore an expression of loneliness and he had a fleeting impression that his uncle was looking at the house through the back of his head. "I'm not looking at anything," he said, but in a moment he turned and looked toward the house again.

"It's a fine snow," Uncle Enid said.

Danny did not answer. He felt the soft, wet touch of the snow against his face as he stared at the house that was receding from them, towing the ponderous landscape with it.

"Good rabbit weather," Uncle Enid said.

Danny looked over the side of the wagon but the thickening carpet of snow was untouched except by the curling foot of the wind. It was snowing hard.

When they had ridden in silence for a long time Uncle Enid pointed to the left and named the dwelling of people who lived miles from the house that until the moment of their departure had been home. Danny followed with his eyes where his uncle pointed; then he turned on the seat, looking homeward.

But the house had receded backward from sight.

10

DANNY

As the wagon wheels unrolled the skein of distance, taking them farther and farther from the house Danny began to look at it in his mind. The first image was clear and sharp, like a photograph. He beheld it as they had left it on setting out. Then he began to approach it as if from the farthest outpost of memory.

At first there was only darkness, not the darkness of night but of not being, of nonexistence. The darkness of the still, essential core, the nothing from which is the root of memory and into which the bough extends. There was stillness in him as he tried to remember, and then motion, but the light did not increase with the death of stillness. It was as if he groped in the unlighted hallway of a house he had known and came up short of the door he was trying to enter, and because the door was not where he remembered it, groped first to the right and then to the left and then without aim in a panic of groping. Once he could have put his hand on the knob of the door in the night.

Or he meant to climb a stair, in darkness still, and went through a hall to the bottom of the stair and lifted his foot and released his weight upon it, and was jarred because his foot had missed the step. His muscles had forgotten their arithmetic. They had forgotten how to add the strides so that the foot was brought on the proper stride to the first step of the stair.

Then the beginning of memory came with a feeling of recognition, as if he came to a landscape he had known before but had not recognized until certain features of it began to speak, began to say hello, speaking the language of familiarity. When he entered the area of memory he progressed as one does along a road that is known, confident, knowing what to look for around the next curve.

So he came to the house.

He could not mistake the house for he issued from it as from the womb of a woman. From it were all his excursions into the random landscapes of memory, the hailed and the un-hailed.

For the house was his mother.

It was a big house and full of rooms. It had been built by an optimistic man who had hoped to people all its rooms and had largely succeeded, though there were six rooms on the first floor and four above stairs. In the history of the house there was a time when all the rooms were inhabited and each room belonged to a person and took on the personality of the person who inhabited it. The people dwelt in their rooms and made excursions from them in their daily living. At intervals one would go away. One by one they went from their rooms and did not return there. They broke from the shells of their rooms like moths from their cocoons and were seen in them no more.

But first some would stay in their rooms a long while without coming forth like ants from the anthill to seek food and do whatever it was their lot to do. They were busy in their rooms, and those who came and went yet carried food into them and came forth again, but the inhabitants did not come out of their rooms. Were they busy there? Were they preparing to leave their rooms forever? Was it hard to leave their rooms?

In the morning of his memory he went through the hall that divided the long end of the L-shaped house from the short end and he passed four doors. The first two on either side of the hall were Nobody's Rooms and the other two belonged to him and to Uncle Enid.

That was after the Old Woman's room became a Nobody's Room. He had looked for her everywhere but she was not to be found. She had slipped like a moth from its cocoon and was gone forever. But she had not gone as all the others had. He remembered her lying on a board between two chairs wrapped in white stuff that clung to her and covered her like the brown wrapping of the moth's cocoon. Later that was gone too. The white stuff must have pinioned wings for when he had looked for her again she had disappeared. Had she taken flight like a great moth toward the candle of the sun?

The floor that was below stairs was given over to the everyday affairs of living, and except to speculate about the Nobody's Rooms it offered little of interest and no hidden crannies to explore that might yield up a treasure like the broken clock he found in the attic. The inhabitants of the rooms above stairs had been gone so long no trace of them remained. The attic was divided into rooms, four in all, with a storage space over the short end of the L unlighted by any window and filled with the castoffs of years.

The attic was a good place to hide from the chores when he had reached the age when boys are expected to cut the wood for the fireplace and bring water from the spring and carry shucks to the livestock in the barn. It was easy to hide there and not be found, for when Uncle Enid was looking for him he came only to the top of the stairs and not finding him in the room the stairs entered, would go down again. In the second or third room from the stairs he was safe from discovery. He would lie on a discarded bed tick filled with its remnants of straw and dream or fall asleep in the dusty motes swimming in the shaft of sun that came warm through a west window.

"I remember the string," he said suddenly, his voice rising against the sound of the wagon wheels upon the road.

"What string?" Uncle Enid said, surprised out of his meditations and long silence.

Then Danny saw the impossibility of making his uncle understand about the string.

"Just a string," he said.

Once while lying on the bed tick in the attic his eyes lighted on a length of string caught on the rough wood of the roof sheeting. It whirled continually in the currents of air moving about the room. He watched it a long time and not even for a moment did it come to rest. He forgot what he went to the attic for that day in watching the string.

Days later he went to the room and the string was in the same position and moved with the same movements as before. It was wonderful about the string. It never rested. Everything in his experience became tired and rested, or if it were moved by an outside force, the force tired and the thing rested. But the string moved continually in the swirling of the air currents.

Several months later he went to the room and the string moved still. He felt in him a pity for the string that never rested, but his admiration for it was greater than his pity and he watched it, fascinated. It occurred to him that he might take the string from where it was caught and leave it on the floor where none of the objects moved, but then it would be an ordinary string and not a thing of delight and fluid motion that never ceased moving in a world of tire and rest.

When he was old enough to think of it in that way the string became for him the metaphor for life.

His memory returned from the string and took up the theme of the Old Woman.

I remember how the Old Woman became my grandmother, he thought.

The Old Woman.

I was alone in the house. I was not in one of the Nobody's Rooms but in the large room in the short end of the L, the one that was used for kitchen and dining room and living room all together. I was without any clothes. I was crying and without my clothes. Why was I without clothes? I was little. I must have messed my pants and removed them because I didn't want to wear them messed. I was naked as the back of my hand. I could not open the clothespress to get more clothes and I cried in the house.

I was alone in the house. I went outside the house and I was crying at the top of my voice outside the house. The sound of my crying went from the house and drifted over the dwelling place of the thing of dread.

He paused in his memory, his thoughts wrecked against the thing of dread. He had forgotten about the thing of dread. It had been a monster that had grown from the tales the others had told him and lived in a cave that was in the bank not far from the house.

It must have been that I was afraid my crying would disturb the thing of dread and lead him to where I cried outside the house. But I was uncomfortable and the figures were in the field and if I cried one of the figures would come to me and do what I wanted of them. They were just figures yet, because I didn't remember them and it was later that the Old Woman working with my Uncle Enid in the field was my grandmother, and it was later that Uncle Enid was Uncle Enid. He was just a figure in the field.

I cried and one of the figures separated from the other and began to come toward me. The figure had to come up a hill because the house was higher than the field and for a while the figure was hid in the fold between the field and the top of the hill where the house was. While the figure was hid I cried the harder because I thought the figure was not coming to me after all. But the figure emerged from the fold of the hill and as it came up first a head was in view and then shoulders and body and legs and feet. And the body was skirted in a black skirt and the feet were in black button shoes and the skirt came down to the tops of them.

I remember how it was.

The figure came to me and took me into the house and soothed me and clothed me and left me pacified. I remember the face. It was an old face, it was like a tanned squirrel skin and the eyes were faded and blue but they were good eyes. When I was pacified she returned to the field, but she was not a figure without features that worked in the field. She was my grandmother and her face was old and her eyes were faded and blue but the eyes never left me again until I came through the hall and all the rooms were Nobody's Rooms except mine and Uncle Enid's and there was not a room that was my grandmother's room.

But there was more about my grandmother.

I had burst Uncle Enid's guitar. He never got another one. I burst it because I was trying to make the good sounds come out of it and did not know how. I was taking the guitar to my uncle so he could make the good sounds come and the guitar was as tall as I and I fell over it and burst it. Uncle Enid was angry with me and his hands trembled and he wished to get a switch and thrash me. I know he did. I could tell. I stood in the presence of his anger and there was no place to hide from it and I stood not knowing what to do but in fear, and my grandmother came and stood behind me and said to Uncle Enid that he was not to touch me. I stood frightened against my grandmother and felt the warmth of her body against me and the warmth of her being flowing about me that the coldness of Uncle Enid's anger could not penetrate. I stood looking at Uncle Enid because he was the one that threatened me. I looked at him to be certain he did not circumvent the safety the presence of my grandmother made about me and punish me still. And he looked back at me. He looked at me intently and strangely with divided eyes.

He shivered in the cold in the wagon.

He had been plunged into such a temperature when the warmth of his grandmother's being had been quenched in the frost of death.

II

DANNY

From his memories he returned to the wagon that rumbled through actual time and the falling snow. It was near sunset and cold and Uncle Enid took a blanket from the back of the wagon and spread it across their laps. The wind came up and blew out of the north, stinging their faces. Danny's feet were numb with cold and he stamped them over the floor of the wagon bed to restore them to feeling.

The sun had been invisible all day but its light had come diffused through the clouds and as it set indefinite shadows grew in the woods along the road. Danny cast fearful glances into their depths but nothing came out of the woods to devour them. They moved slowly through the falling dusk and the fallen snow.

Uncle Enid began hurrying the mare and Danny wondered where they were going to stop for the night. They had come a distance of seven or eight miles since setting out at noon. He was not familiar with the road over which they were passing. He had not been over it in a long time.

"There's an old house at the Gap," Uncle Enid said as if in answer to his questioning of himself. "And a barn. We can put the mare in the stable and sleep in the house. It will be better than sleeping in the wagon. We can build a fire."

The gap of which he spoke was a low opening in the mountain range that divided their valley from more open country to the north. A family had once lived there, farming the gentler levels of the hills that rose from the gap through which the road snaked in crooks and turns like the path of a rattler fleeing the hills.

Danny said nothing, he was cold and sleep was drawing

about him like darkness with voices. He leaned against Uncle Enid. He wanted to lie in his lap.

"It's not far now," Uncle Enid said.

The stone of sleep was upon Danny's tongue. He said nothing, but the jolting of the wagon roused him and he turned on the seat and looked back down the valley. They were rounding a curve and he could see far down the valley whence they had come. In its covering of snow it lay open and light at the base of a greater darkness that was the sky.

"Here we are," Uncle Enid said, and looking ahead Danny could see the dark tongue of sky licking the cleft in the hills.

When they had fed the mare and cooked their own meal over the open fire they made a pallet of quilts and went to bed in their clothes. They lay as close together as they could and the warmth of his uncle's body enclosed Danny in a comfortable shell. He could hear voices speaking to him. From sleep the voices were asking him something but the moment after they had spoken he forgot what it was they asked. He meant to ask Uncle Enid what the voices said but instead he slept.

When he was asleep he was again in his bed in the house where he was born. In sleep he outwitted the dislocations he had suffered in the day. In that beneficent weather all things grew whole.

12

DANNY

In the night Danny woke. The moon was up making the world outside glisten. It had stopped snowing but when the wind blew a fine spray of snow came through the roof and settled on his face. The cover had slipped and even when he lay as close as he could to Uncle Enid it did not meet the floor. His whole side was cold, it felt like a steel crowbar lying against the rest of his body.

"I'm cold," he said.

His words dropped into silence like stones into deep water. Uncle Enid was not awake. He was afraid to be awake alone in the strangeness of the old house. He shuffled against his uncle who grunted in his sleep, making sounds like a cow, and then his head snapped up and he asked Danny what it was he had said.

"I'm cold," Danny said again.

Uncle Enid shifted his position and tucked the cover over him as he had always done when Danny slept alone in the house they had left. Danny nestled against him, fitting his cold side to the warmth of the quilt where his uncle had lain. Lying so close to his uncle he was embarrassed but it was good to be warm and he lay still.

He could not return to sleep. The thicket of sleep grew all about him but he could not creep within it again. He lay wakeful staring through the broken window that looked out on the white world outside. He asked Uncle Enid when they could get up and his uncle looked at his watch by the moon-light pouring through the window.

"It's three o'clock," he said, "go to sleep. It's a long while till time to get up."

He was afraid of the silence when the wind did not blow. From deep in him he remembered the absolute silence that followed the cry of *fire!* before the blasts went off when his uncle had blasted stumps from the fields. In his mind he saw the earth outside rise up and then collapse upon itself with a shuddering crash.

"What if the world blew up?" he said.

"It won't," Uncle Enid said. He laughed. His laughter had a muffled and distorted sound as if his mouth were full of cotton.

"But what if somebody had put dynamite at the center of the world and lighted a long fuse?" Danny persisted.

"It would be too bad," Uncle Enid said.

"Bessie would blow up too, wouldn't she? And the bull and Old Five-Pigs?"

"I guess so," Uncle Enid said.

"Would we blow up?" Danny said.

"Sure," Uncle Enid said. He slurred the word, wavering its outline because he spoke it through a yawn.

Danny was silent for a while but when he heard his uncle breathing hard again he was full of panic and began to send his voice out into the silence of the ghostly house. When he first slept there had been something on his mind, troubling but unformulated. Perhaps that was why he had wakened. Now he began to phrase it.

"Will the snow be gone when we come back?" he said.

"I don't know," Uncle Enid said. His voice was fully wakened, cautious.

"When are we coming back?"

"I don't know that, either."

"Tomorrow?"

"No," Uncle Enid said.

"Day after tomorrow?"

"No," Uncle Enid said. Then he spoke his nephew's name as if he were not certain where he was.

"What?" Danny said.

"We are not coming back," Uncle Enid said. His voice was matter-of-fact, as if by his simple statement he had settled everything satisfactorily.

"Not ever?"

"Not ever."

"Why?" Danny said in the same tone he asked why he might not do something he had been forbidden to do.

"I sold the place," Uncle Enid said. "I thought you knew that."

"I did," Danny said, "I knew you sold it but I didn't think that meant we couldn't ever go back."

"What else could it mean?" Uncle Enid said.

Danny lay in silence but until he slept again a rabbit without a burrow was in his mind, and a bird without a nest.

13

UNCLE ENID

Now that he came to assess them, lying on a temporary pallet in an abandoned house, the reasons for his leaving the place of his birth began to emerge clearly into his consciousness. He realized dimly that the two forces that drove him arose from the same source. The flight from solitude, the search for love, these, he saw, grew out of his aloneness, except for the boy who alone was with him and whom alone he loved, at the farm that seemed at the distance of a day's journey already incredibly far and lost in a cup of the hills.

Sensing in Danny the reluctance of the young bird to fly the nest he came to think of him as a fledgling sparrow lost in the wide woods, and a feeling of warmth and pity that transcended and bridged the gap the gold piece made between them went out to him, but himself he came to think of as a hawk risen from the same tree in quest.

He was in flight before time.

When youth, like a May day, was over he became acutely aware of the meaning of time's passing. It was as if a thief stole from his inheritance before he came to possess it. The inheritance menaced by the thieving fingers included love. He needed the love of a woman. He needed it while he was young and handsome enough to win it. If he should wait till middle age overtook him he could still find a marriage partner, but he would have to take the leavings of other men, he would have to take second choice or marry at a bargain. It was against his nature to accept what other men scorned.

Therefore he was in a great hurry to find love before time had stolen his capacity to win it. He felt within himself that the thieving fingers fumbled at that particular treasure.

As he thought of the love of a woman the arm he had rested lightly about Danny's body to comfort his sleep tightened. When at last sleep came to him again that magician transformed Danny's body into the anomalous but unmistakably feminine form imaged in the retina of his desires.

14

Before setting out from the Gap on the second day of their journey Uncle Enid looked back into the valley and he could see the bald face of a new ground on the farm that had been his own. As he looked at it, taking farewell, Danny peered into his face and he thought suddenly he could see all the farm lying in his uncle's eyes, the barn and the house and the animals and the land itself lying there in his eyes.

When they set out their faces were toward the unknown. Looking from the Gap the way they had come the country lay dear and familiar. They could name the farms to which the fields they could see over the countryside belonged. But when they looked ahead all that met their eyes was a strange country, spurs and valleys their feet had never walked upon. Yet the power with which the unfamiliar landscape reached out and gripped them was due to its strangeness. They were impatient to descend from the Gap into the depth of the unknown country.

The road dropped away from the Gap in a steep incline. The mare moved forward slowly, planting her feet carefully in the slippery snow. In a little while they had dropped below the open spaces of the Gap and were driving through an avenue of trees that stood upon each side of the road, bowed under their white weight and still as posts set in cement. The landscape visible to them at times through breaks in the forest wall was an etching in black and white. The mountain range on the far horizon, heaved brokenly up from the plain, stood with every ridge and valley plainly outlined, resembling in its features the path of a monstrous mole.

The mountain gave way after a while to a valley. The road ran through the bottom of the valley and at length it was companioned by a small stream bridged at intervals by snow-laden limbs that had fallen from the trees. Now and then the snow slipped from one of these bridges and disappeared into the black water of the stream with a little hiss.

Uncle Enid sang to himself as the wagon moved on:

> "Black is the color of my true love's hair,
> Her lips are something wondrous fair.
> If she on earth no more I see
> My life will quickly fade away."

The pathos of the song rode in his voice as if it belonged there, he lacking a truelove, he lacking a love of his own to sing about.

At intervals Danny was conscious of a phrase of what his uncle was singing. The newness of the valley kept him looking from side to side, moving his head with the agility of a person dodging stones. They had passed beyond the limits of his knowledge of the country at the Gap. They were well into the unknown and the possibilities before them accounted for the holiday look Uncle Enid noted in his nephew's eyes.

Even a journey in a strange country becomes tedious and Danny began to fidget as the morning wore away. He began to explore his mind for something strange to beguile the journey. He went back in his mind and the bars to memory fell one by one until he came to a point and there the bars did not fall.

"Tell me about when I was little," he said to his uncle.

"What?" Uncle Enid said, and Danny saw that his uncle

had forgotten the moment of time they traversed also. His gaze was withdrawn from the snowy landscape, looking inward.

"Tell me about when I was little," Danny said again.

"When you were little?" Uncle Enid said as if he returned from an absence.

"Yes," Danny said.

"Well, I guess you remember most of it," Uncle Enid said, reluctant now to re-enter forgotten time and censor the past for the boy by his side.

"I remember the house," Danny said. "I remember me in the house. I was there in the house a long time before anybody else was there."

"Well, no," Uncle Enid said.

"Tell me," Danny said, "who else was there?"

"Your mother, your grandmother and me."

"I remember the house," Danny said again. He was seeing it as they had left it a short while before, for his knowledge of the house was continuous, unbroken from the time of his first memory to the moment of their departure.

"Tell me about it, when I was little."

"Ah now," Uncle Enid said, slapping the lines against the mare's back, "there was your mother and your grandmother and me. That's about all."

"I remember my grandmother," Danny said, "I remember her. I don't remember my mother."

"No," Uncle Enid said, "you was just tiny when she died."

"Tell me about my mother," Danny said.

"Your mother was a flower," Uncle Enid said. A shadow crossed his face and his voice darkened. I'll not tell him, he thought. After all these years. If I never tell him. But he himself was remembering:

He hated the child Danny and as he rode in the wagon he

was seeing again the ugly and infant-new face of the child that, born out of wedlock, was less welcome in the world than the whelp of a sheep-killing bitch dropped in a shuckpen. He looked at the fresh boy face of his nephew beside him with its clear profile that was beginning to render unto the Caesar of blood the due of family likeness. He had the clear and beautiful features of his mother Daisy who died before he had been six weeks in the world. She had borne six weeks the fact of her disgrace and then turned her face to the wall and died.

He had hated the child because he had robbed him of his sister. But first he had hated his sister because through her disgrace she had brought about the fall of his pride. The vision of the young Danny dissolved in his mind and he was remembering again the night of his begetting. The hand of his mother materialized through the wall of years to shake his shoulder.

He had been lying in bed asleep.

"What?" he said when his mother touched him.

"Get up, Enid," she said. "It's Daisy." Anxiety was in her voice, slurring it. He was unsure of the identity of the voice coming to him, slurred, and diluted by its seepage through the wall of sleep.

He heard the shape of the words and then their meaning. When they penetrated his mind it was as if he were hearing them a second time long after they were spoken.

"Get up! get up!" his mother said, "it's Daisy."

His head emerged from between the covers like an inquisitive turtle's.

"Oh," he said. "It's still dark. What is it?"

"It's Daisy," his mother said. "It's two-thirty."

Two-thirty. He expected the full light of day. He blinked against the light his mother had placed on the bureau, rubbing his eyes with his hand. When he was oriented on the proper side of midnight his brain slipped into focus, and he looked at his mother standing there, staring at him, anxiety hunching her head forward like a fighter's.

"Where's the Flower?" he said. "Is she home yet? What is it?" He had always called Daisy the Flower because of her name.

"She's not here," his mother said. "Something's wrong. It's two-thirty in the morning."

At that moment a strange thing happened. He had a premonition about his sister. It struck him with a shock and he put it down to his suspicious nature. He had a premonition that the Flower was beginning to wither.

He rose, his back to his mother, and began drawing on his clothes.

Daisy had gone to the Glade, the church not far away. She was attending a singing school there. She had gone by herself, while it was still light. They expected a beau to escort her home. What was there to worry about?

Yet it was two-thirty in the morning.

"Maybe she's staying with Marge," he said, naming a friend of Daisy's.

"No," his mother said, "she would have told me. Go see."

He was already dressing. And already it was like a hunt. He took a pistol from the bureau. Its steel barrel glinted in the light from the lamp.

His mother brought her hand to her cheek and stared at the gun. "No," she said, her eyes on the gun, "don't take that."

"Why?" he said.

"Don't take it," she said again without giving reason, "don't take that."

He tossed the pistol back on the bureau. It held his eyes still when he went from the room. He stepped outside. It was almost as light as day. The moon was the span of his hand above the western horizon.

He stepped into the road. Anxiety and an undefinable anger grew in him as he went from the house. Before he had gone far Buster, his hound, came at his heels. He learned of the dog's presence when he struck his nose with his heel in lifting his foot for a stride. He whirled, startled, his nerves taut. Buster sat in the road, thrown back by surprise, beating the erratic drum of his tail.

His fingers touched the dog. "Silent, boy," he said, and Buster came with him, came like an equal by his side, alert, searching the sides of the road with his nostrils, his ears forward like broken tobacco leaves, the fur over his powerful shoulders rippling in the moonlight that came splotched through the overhanging foliage.

What had he been thinking? He had had no feeling that danger menaced either Daisy or himself. His fear, for he was afraid, was of something insidious. Was the Flower beginning to wither? He was young then, had come that summer to his majority. He was young and strong and prideful. He looked at the world with a stare of defiance that fed upon his pride. Was he afraid the downfall of his pride waited ahead of him, lurked in the night, bound up with the person and fate of Daisy?

Daisy should not be out at two-thirty in the morning with a beau. People would talk. What was Daisy thinking? Daisy was his sister. The sisters of other men might, but before God, if Daisy ever did.

Something must have happened to Daisy. What?

She could not have fallen from a footlog and been hurt, as had happened to a neighbor once; there was no stream to cross between the house and the church where the singing school was held. It was only a little better than a mile, and two houses between. Had she been taken sick on the way?

Daisy and a beau.

Damn these singing schools and their so me do's, he thought. A man up at two-thirty in the morning looking for his sister because of a singing school. He was thinking of the teacher. He did not know him, had seen him only once, the first night of the school which he had attended himself. It was generally held that there were three classes of men. Honest men, thieves and singing-school teachers.

If Daisy hadn't found a beau.

But she always had found a beau. She could take her pick and choice. He had been proud of her for that. She was a beautiful girl. Their fa la so me re do's he thought angrily.

He recognized her voice even before it had completed a word.

"Buster?" it said.

And, "Buster!"

Then, "It's Buster! Someone's coming!"

The voice was low, startled. There was the sound of scurrying, snapping of twigs as if someone rose. The dog that had just been at his side barked happy, low sounds of recognition beyond the bushes at the road's edge. He stopped dead in his tracks. A gust of trembling went through his body.

Daisy's voice came through the wall of bushes, beginning a sob of anxiety that died into silence. He was through the wall of undergrowth with a bound, among them, Daisy, the hound, and a stranger he had never seen before. Daisy screamed when she saw him, her hand over her mouth, the heel of her hand against her chin. The cup of her hand funneled the cry in a thin eeeeee upward. It passed, a disbodied sound, lost, and thin, over the trees around the natural bower into which the moonlight streamed.

The stranger was poised for flight. His body strained forward from the waist, away from him, yet the stranger stood rooted, his clothes in disarray, his face half hidden in the uncertain light. He had the stranger's collar in his left hand, his right poised back of his shoulder in a fist. In a moment he would crash his fist into the face. The face was expressionless in the moonlight, the mouth slightly open. He supported part of the stranger's weight with his hand at the collar, the body was going limp. He lifted him to his full height and held him trembling in his grasp.

Suddenly the flesh in the stranger's right cheek began to twitch. It danced a jig like a leaf in a fluttery wind. A strange sensation took him as he looked at the twitching flesh, pale and ghost-colored in the moonlight. Revulsion shook him, as if he held something monstrous. He struck the face with all the power he had in his right arm. The blow knocked the stranger from his grasp, leaving part of the shirt collar in his hand.

The stranger fell through the wall of light. He fell into darkness at the bower's edge. Before he could lay hands on him again the stranger was on his feet and in flight, running in the dark woods, running, running, the sound of his feet like the sound of a startled buck in flight. He gave chase as long as he could judge the direction of the stranger by the sound of his footsteps. At length he stopped to listen, and a silence greeted him. A silence dead and absolute came up to meet him like a tide.

Daisy was gone when he returned to the bower. She had run home, the dog with her, the dog by her side loving, not judging her.

Because he swore to kill him Daisy would not tell him the stranger's name. He asked in the community and learned that the stranger was a friend of the singing-school teacher, had come with him from the next county, but because his vow had traveled ahead of him no one would tell him his name, nor give him any other clue to his identity.

Yet the twitching cheek would serve to mark him for revenge should he meet the stranger, even in hell.

He emerged from the memory sapped of energy. He touched the boy that had grown from the infant of his memory, his touch carrying forgiveness for his part in the tragedy of which he was the cause but blameless.

"Your mother was a flower," he said, "just a flower that withered early."

By midafternoon they were passing through country that was more thickly settled. There had been only solitary huts set far apart in the lean land of the mountain's flank. Now the houses stood at intervals of a mile or so, good substantial houses that spoke of the richness of the land lying in narrow strips along the creek that had fed the rich loam from the mountains to the sandy-clay soil until it had grown fat. The dead cornstalks of the autumn harvest stood yet in rows, marching the length of the fields. One field they passed had not been harvested and Uncle Enid said the man was lazy or ailing, else he would have gathered his corn long ago.

But the corn makes crows, Danny thought, looking at the shadows of the ears black against the snow. When the man gathers his corn, he thought idly, the crows will fly the field.

The day had been filled with the barking of dogs and an occasional hail from the people of the houses they had passed. The loneliness they had felt in the passage through the Gap was dissipated by these friendly sounds. When the dripping from the trees became discouraged and then ceased altogether in the cold of returning night they made camp by the road and the presence of people near warmed them like the flame of the fire they kindled of brush.

15

The second night of the journey they slept in the wagon. They cleared the wagon bed and placed quilts on the floor and slept between them with all their clothes on.

"You had better keep them on," Uncle Enid said when Danny began to remove his shoes.

"Why?" Danny said.

"You might stick your feet from under the cover in your sleep."

"What would happen to them?" Danny said.

"They might get frostbitten," Uncle Enid said.

"What would they look like if they got frostbitten?"

"They would be black and sore."

"They are black already," Danny said.

"That's because you haven't washed them."

"But they are not sore," Danny said.

"No," Uncle Enid said, "but you ought to wash your feet."

"It's too much trouble," Danny said, "besides nobody sees them like they do your face."

"But they stink, I can smell them through your shoes," Uncle Enid said, and he made a loud sniffing sound.

"You can't smell them," Danny said. He moved his toes inside his shoes. They were as cold as pellets of ice.

"Let me pull off my shoes and warm my feet," he said.

"What in the name of common sense do you think you would warm them on?"

"I could scrooch them up. I could warm them with my hands."

"I'm not holding you," Uncle Enid said, "but don't get the covers off."

Danny removed his shoes and then placed his bare feet

against Uncle Enid's legs where they were bare between the bottom of his trousers and his shoe tops.

"Holy Jesus!" Uncle Enid said, "you are colder than a frog."

"How cold's a frog?" Danny said.

"Anybody knows how cold a frog is," Uncle Enid said.

Sound flowed over the edge of the wagon bed like water over a dam. The sound of the snow-laden trees moving gently to the wind and the tramping sound the mare made as she moved around the tree where she was tethered came flowing over the wagon bed. When Danny lay on his back and looked straight into the sky it did not look far. If he looked at one star long enough space circled in a widening funnel from the star to his eyes. It was like looking up a tall cylinder from a dark place into light far at the top. The funnel poured loneliness upon him. It tapped the dams of space and the loneliness from space came pouring down upon him.

Uncle Enid's breathing was regular and quiet. Danny lifted his head and looked over the edge of the sideboards. Darkness lay all about, deep and undisturbed. Beyond the sounds of the mare's hoofs lay the edge of the world. He pulled the covers over his head and put his arm across Uncle Enid's chest which rose and fell with the coming and going of his breath.

"What were you scared of?" Uncle Enid said.

"Nothing," Danny said, withdrawing his arm.

"You were afraid something would come and get you, weren't you?"

"No," Danny said.

"There's nothing out there to get you," Uncle Enid said.

"No," Danny said, "there's nothing out there to hurt a body."

"Don't be afraid of anything but a man," Uncle Enid said. "Man is the meanest animal of all."

Danny said nothing, lacking conviction, lacking experience to judge.

"Not all men are mean," Uncle Enid said, "but a mean man is the meanest thing in the world. He'll do anything under the shining sun."

"Yes," Danny said fitting his body into the crook Uncle Enid's body made. At length he heard his voice again breaking through the edges of sleep.

"Danny," he was saying, "we won't go back to the big house any more."

"No," Danny said.

"I may have to board you out somewhere for a while."

"I don't want you to," Danny said.

"I know," Uncle Enid said, "but I may have to."

"Why?" Danny said.

"I'll have to find work so we can live."

"I want to go wherever you go," Danny said.

"Yes, but I may have to board you out for a while."

"How long?" Danny said sleepily.

"Oh, not long," Uncle Enid said. Then, influenced by their togetherness in the wagon, by the tearing out of their roots from the farm, by the greatness of the night about them, he said, "I'll tell you something, Danny, you are the only person I've got. I won't ever leave you."

"I won't leave you either," Danny said.

"Remember that," Uncle Enid said.

"I'll remember," Danny said, his words distorted and blown shapeless by the wind of sleep, "I'll remember it."

16

Danny craned his neck and looked up at the woman. She sat on his right, stooped slightly at the shoulders because there was no support for her back on the narrow wagon seat. He thought if he should place his hands in the small of her back where it arched under the weight of her shoulders and push it would increase her height by inches. Her hands, gloved in kid leather, lay together in her lap, loosely and almost in the attitude of prayer. Now and then she was forced to brace herself against the swaying of the wagon; this she did unhurriedly and when danger of sliding from the seat was past she returned her hands to her lap with the palms cradled solemnly together.

She had been riding with them since early in the morning. About eight o'clock they rounded a curve and saw before them a house of singular appearance. Its gable end presented the countenance of a four-eyed face. The gable end had a door in the center which served for the giant's mouth, there were two windows on the first floor, one on either side of the entrance and a little above it. The second pair of eyes looked from the upper story. Snow hung over the eaves like ragged tassels of untended hair. The house stood several yards from the road. They could not see the front of the house from the angle of their approach.

Before they came up to the house two women, who must have been watching their approach from the lower eyes of the giant, issued from the giant's mouth and stood waiting by the side of the road. The younger of the two women was dressed for travel, a great blue coat boxing her figure. The other woman wore a scanty brown sweater and an earth-colored apron, dyed with walnut shells. The two women bore a remarkable resemblance to each other, and at first the two in the wagon assumed they were mother and daughter, but on closer approach the difference in their ages appeared less. They were sisters surely. The older woman's hands were folded in her apron, she stood shivering in the cold. Her sweater was too light for the weather.

They stood with the expectancy of people who wait for others stiffening the planes of their faces. The younger woman was handsome. Her face, full and oval, was kindly and pleasing. Her eyes were reserved but not distant. Her hair was dark and her skin had a slight patina of darkness, like the shine upon good polished wood.

The woman in the sweater stepped forward as the wagon came abreast of them. She said nothing but they could tell from her attitude that she wished them to stop. Uncle Enid drew back on the reins and spoke gently to the mare. She stopped and stood docile between the shafts.

"Good morning," Uncle Enid said. The women were looking at them as if disappointed.

The women did not return the greeting. The younger smiled embarrassedly and the older said in confusion:

"We, ah, thought Mary here might ride a ways with you." She looked questioningly at the younger woman.

"No," the younger woman said, "I thought perhaps your wife . . ." her words died away and she looked searchingly into the wagon as if she might discover another rider there, a woman.

"But the child," the older woman said, "with the child. . . ."

"You are welcome to ride with us," Uncle Enid said, "as far as we go in your direction."

Danny stared at the older woman who smiled at him warmly. He did not know what she meant by her words but he felt that they were complimentary and when she supplemented the words with her smile he felt himself warming toward the stooping woman in the earth-colored apron. When he looked at her again he had dropped the bars that kept strangers out of his eyes.

"Maybe another wagon will be along directly," the younger woman said doubtfully. "It's early yet." Uncle Enid sat waiting for her to decide. He felt no anger or resentment at the implication expressed in her attitude. It was not custom for men and women to ride together unchaperoned.

"With the boy . . ." the older woman was saying. She looked up the road whence they had come. Their wheel tracks were deep cuts in the snow. "There won't be much traveling this day," she said to the younger woman, "with the snow and all."

Uncle Enid began to make room on the seat. He moved as far as he could to the left and pulled Danny against him, leaving ample room for the woman.

"He might not be going by our place," the younger woman said. And she flushed as if forgetting to inquire about this fact at first were a comment upon her intelligence.

"Well," Uncle Enid said, "we are going to the Smelters. That is, if we don't find work before we get there. We are foot-loose now you might say. Just traveling."

The face of the older woman brightened.

"You see!" she said to the other, "they'll have to pass by your door, right by the door."

The younger woman turned as if to go to the house again, and the other began speaking hurriedly.

"I wish you could stay," she said to the younger woman. Then she turned to the two in the wagon. "My sister here, she hasn't been to visit me before in seven years. It does seem that when a family is broken up, scattered all over like, they see each other too seldom."

She spoke to the younger woman:

"I do wish you could stay. But if you are worried about the ones at home . . . I know how it is. Abner is no cook, and the Preacher's mother, she's old. Of course the Preacher hasn't time to take care of the house. And they go right by the door. "And with the child . . ." she finished.

"Yes," the younger woman said to all this, smiling at her sister. "I'll get my bundle."

She was lost to sight by way of the giant's mouth. She returned in a moment carrying a flour sack stuffed until it resembled a fat toad. Uncle Enid hopped nimbly to the ground and took the bundle from her and placed it with their own provisions. Then he held out his hand and the woman placed her hand in his and stepped to the brake block and then to the step on the wagon bed. As she stepped over the sideboards her skirt lifted briefly above her knees and she fought it down with such energy she almost fell from the wagon. Uncle Enid grasped her arm firmly until she was safely seated. Then he climbed to his own place and spoke to the mare. The snow crunched softly under the wheels as they set out again.

The woman turned after a while and waved to the woman in the earth-colored apron, who stood by the road before her house and watched them until they were out of sight.

They completely filled the narrow seat. Danny was pressed in between them, between the man and woman. The animal warmth of their bodies filtered through their clothing and touched him on either side. There was something disturbing about the warmth of their bodies.

Suddenly he thought of the possible thing between them. The touch of flesh.

The blood in his head churned when he thought of it. A sense of shame threaded his feelings, for he was not supposed to be thinking about it. He was not even supposed to know about the possible thing. But he knew. He had heard about it from other boys in the dark. Lying by his side in the dark they had whispered into his ears the dark secret thing between a man and a woman. He had culled it from the coarse jokes he had heard at the mill and in the fields when he and Uncle Enid visited with their neighbors and there were no women present to censor their speech. He had sensed it in the urges that had begun to visit his own body, the urge to complete himself upon another in a mysterious union that was suggested by his own hands lying open on his thighs.

The touch of flesh.

He squirmed on the seat between the man and woman.

"Are you scrouged?" Uncle Enid said.

He did not answer, or move then. He rebelled against a suggestion he sensed in his uncle's voice.

The words between them flew like bees over his head. They had not talked much on starting out. The woman had answered Uncle Enid's questions but put none of her own. Said Mary when Uncle Enid asked her her name, though he knew it already from the other woman. Said Mervin when asked her husband's name. Said two when asked the number of her children. Said Jason and Ezra when asked their names. Said the Preacher, her husband, owned a great farm of a hundred acres of bottom land. Said Abner managed the farm when her husband was absent, as he frequently was attending his churches. Said Abner was a good man, the biggest man they ever saw, but a poor manager. Said a hundred things, her calm, unanxious voice issuing slowly from her lips while she looked at her kid-gloved hands lying solemnly together palm to palm.

Then she had begun to talk of her own accord, warming to them as the distance crept behind them, flowing backward from the wagon bed. She asked them of their past lives at the farm, and of their plans for the future.

"I thought I'd work awhile at the Smelters," Uncle Enid said, referring to the copper smelter in the edge of the next state, the only industrial plant in a hundred miles. "It was lonely there on the farm, you don't know how lonely. Mostly nobody but me and the boy for weeks at a time. I had a mighty good farm," he said, pride in his voice until he remembered he had sold it, then his voice fell a little but lifted again as he continued, "got a pretty good price for it, even if we did have to move out in the middle of the winter with no place to go."

He thought of the gold piece then for the first time on the third day of their journey. It appeared in his imagination a moment, round and golden. And then it bore suddenly the image of the woman in the wagon.

"They pay mighty well at the Smelters," he said after a while, "I hear they pay a dollar and a quarter a day." He said it in a voice filled with wonder. In the cornfields or ground-hogging stumps from the new grounds a man earned fifty cents a day.

Danny squirmed between them. The warmth of their flesh burned against him on either side. It enveloped him and he breathed it into his lungs like the hot, humid air of July.

"You could sit on the floor if you are scrouged," Uncle Enid said, making explicit the suggestion that had been in his voice before.

Still he did not move.

"The only trouble with me working at the Smelters," Uncle Enid said to the woman, "there's got to be a place for the boy. I don't want to take him into a boardinghouse where there are a lot of workers staying. They tell me there are some pretty tough customers working at the Smelters. Living in a boardinghouse with them might be a bad influence for the boy."

After he had drawn sharply on the lines to avoid a deep hole in the road he continued, "Besides, there'd be nothing for him to do. I don't believe in bringing a boy up in idleness."

The wagon jolted and Danny slipped against the woman, buried into her ample side, and she placed her arm around him for a moment and smiled at him. Her face grew motherly and was shut for a moment of the indefinable hunger that marked it.

"He could stay with us," Mary said. "We have room for him in the house. He could help in the fields." And she began to tell them of the farm and of her family and as she talked they could see them growing like visions out of her words.

They saw a farm of a hundred acres of bottom land that belonged to the Preacher. He had inherited it from his father. The Preacher had worked the farm, piling up wealth of money and livestock and grains for four years.

"That was before he heard the Call," Mary said. "It was different afterward. There wasn't much time left for the farm after he became the pastor of eight churches. The churches are scattered here and yon. It takes him a day to ride between some of them.

"It was funny about the Call," she said, searching her mind. "He had always been content to work the farm until three or four years after Jason, my oldest, was born. I was carrying Ezra," she said as naturally as if she had said the cow had calved, "I sometimes think that is why he is simple. The worry the Preacher caused us.

"It was near my time and one day the Preacher disappeared. We were frantic, my mother-in-law Mercidy and I; we sent out neighbors to search but nothing came of it. He was gone four days.

"On the fourth day he returned. I looked up one day and he was standing in the door. He never said where he had been. But he had got the Call while he was away. His face was bruised like he had fallen. He was in a trance when he got the Call, he said. He was in a trance and must have fallen.

"Mercidy was proud," she said after a pause, "when he stood before the people with the word of God in his mouth she was proud."

She was silent for a while and then she said,

"After that he found Abner to work the farm. He's as strong as an ox but slow in his mind. He is like one of the family. We set great store by Abner.

"He is a good man, the Preacher," she said, her eyes round and troubled in her dark face, "a good man," and looked before her.

She began to make them acquainted with the other members of her household.

"There is Jason. He is turning sixteen soon. He is good to his brother."

She paused and her breath came and went, heaving her ample bosom.

"Ezra is simple," she said. "I sometimes think that is what caused it, my worry over the Preacher. Jason is good to his brother Ezra. Jason is a good boy."

They rode in silence for a while. The snow fell away from the boughs, splattering wetly under the trees.

"The only other person in the house is Mercidy," Mary said, "my mother-in-law. She is old but strong yet. She is the mainstay of the Preacher. She is proud of him because he stands before the people."

After a while she turned and looked at Danny, smiling. "We have room for the boy," she said. "We have room for him in the house."

Danny slipped from between them and crawled under the wagon seat and lay on a quilt on the wagon bed. The landscape moved by him, clipped from its base by the sideboards of the wagon. He saw the mountains without base and the trees that dripped in the warming day and the cloud-flecked sky moving along the edge of the wagon bed, moving past him, racing behind him to their ultimate destination in chaotic memory.

The sky is a high place, he thought. And he thought of other high places, the cliff that rose from the creek's edge on the farm they had left, the long white oaks in the thicket to the east of the barn, and the barn itself. He was strangely moved and delighted when he thought of them.

The bird in my head can fly from the high places, he thought. I am not afraid of high places. When I was first in a tree, a little way up, the soles of my feet tingled and I hugged the tree in fright and the bird of my head did not fly. I came down again.

But I climbed other trees. I climbed the pippin in the field. It was a high tree and I climbed as high as I could. I climbed till the water sprout that bore the apples bent under my weight. I picked the apples, the yellowest ones because those that are green are no good yet, and I came down again. The bird of my head flew from the pippin tree.

I was with Dyer in the white oak thicket. We were lying in the leaves. Let's climb a tree and bend out, Dyer said. No I said. You are afraid Dyer said. No I said I am not afraid. I was not afraid to climb the tree. But I did not want to cling with my hands and let my feet go in space. The bird in my head would not fly if my feet left the tree. There would be too much confusion in my head for the bird to fly.

I am going to bend out Dyer said. He looked at me. But I was shut out of his eyes. If I did not climb a tree and bend out he would not let me into his eyes again. He climbed a tall tree. He climbed to the topmost branch and he swung with his weight a few times to set the tree in motion, and then he clung with his hands and let go with his feet and the tree began to bend. It let him to the ground in an easy sweep. He rested on the balls of his feet and swayed and looked at me and then he climbed again.

I climbed a tree of my own. I climbed to the top of the tree but it looked too high to swing out. I rested in the tree.

You are afraid to swing out Dyer said.

I am not afraid I said. I got a good grip on the tree. I let my feet swing free. I drifted gently through the air and the bird in my head flew better than ever. When I reached the ground he had unlocked his eyes.

We will swing one together Dyer said.

I remember once at the barn. I wanted on the scaffold where Uncle Enid was fixing the barn. He didn't want me there. It's dangerous he said. I am not afraid I said I like to be high. You stay on the ground he said. I want on the scaffold I said. I'll hand you nails.

The place looked strange from the scaffold. I could see all over the place like from a mountain. I could look down on the hog lot and see the sow and the pigs. I could look into the field on the far side of the house that you couldn't see from the ground because there were trees between. I could look into the south pasture. I could see the specks of blue that the sky made in the puddles of water dammed behind sticks in the branch. The pasture was good. The grass was even like a blanket except where it humped over the little rises in the ground. That looked like it covered somebody asleep. I could see the queens of the meadow purple by the branch. The cow was on the far side of the pasture. She looked like a toy play cow. The fence was no higher than my finger.

I was too far out on the board we used for a scaffold. I felt the board give under me. Fear flew to my stomach. I looked toward Uncle Enid. His foot was resting on the board. He must have shifted his weight for a minute. The board felt solid again and I looked into his face to see if he knew I nearly fell and would make me get down from the scaffold. He was looking at me and while he looked at me something happened in his eyes. The two ways of his looking at me flew together and he looked at me with undivided eyes. I moved closer to him on the scaffold and the bird of my head flew farther from the scaffold than it did from the pippin tree.

She had removed her glove and her hand rested on the seat between them, bracing her against the pitching of the wagon; and Uncle Enid, bracing himself, rested his hand on the seat also. Their hands touched.

The touch of flesh.

Danny watched them from his pallet in the back of the wagon. For a moment there was a strange sensation in his middle, as if his flesh knew of more than his mind. The sensation was gone suddenly and he lay quietly in the back of the wagon, watching them.

Somewhere on the road the wagon tilted, throwing them against each other. When it straightened again they did not move apart but sat against each other, their bodies touching.

He had learned about it from the coarse mouths of the men joking in the fields. He watched them repelled and fascinated.

In the afternoon they stopped to make a fire.

"Hold the lines," Uncle Enid said, giving him the reins. "We will go and find a brush heap. The wood under the brush will be dry."

"Tie the mare," Danny said. He did not want to hold her.

"You can tie her while we are gone," Uncle Enid said.

Mary stood hesitant and he turned and looked at her and she went with him.

When they returned later it was written in their faces. They could not declare, even to his supposed unknowing, that the thing possible between them had not been accomplished. Seeing them coming from the woods Danny remembered, and with the fleeting sense that he had betrayed her, the woman in the earth-colored apron.

Later he remembered Mary's eagerness to resume the homeward journey. His next recollection was of seeing Ezra and Jason, whom he recognized from their mother's description, standing by the road to see who came with their mother in a strange wagon.

17

Their journey was over. The indifferent earth would hold no memory of it, for in all the distance they had not touched it. The snow bore their weight and cushioned the earth from the mark of their wheels. When it melted and ran into the streams and soaked into the ground the sign of their journey would vanish from the face of the earth forever. Thinking that their faring was almost as if it had not been Uncle Enid was nostalgic for a moment for the little memorial of the mark of feet upon the ground. Only in his heart and mind would the journey, made memorable by the presence of the woman in their wagon, endure with the tenacity of the imprint of his foot upon the mountains of home.

He thought once more of the gold piece, and because it bore now the image of the woman it was removed from between his nephew and himself and never again did it lie between them.

18

The Preacher made Uncle Enid overseer of his hundred acres in Abner's stead, and though he still dreamed of going to the Smelters to work and promised himself that this was only a pause on the way, they stayed at the Preacher's that winter.

PART III

THE TIME OF THE HIGH SUN

DANNY

They could see the figure at the well from where they worked in the field a distance from the house. The figure had come from the kitchen bearing an earthen jug that tugged at her arm and seemed to bend her body toward the ground. In her progress from the kitchen door to the well she passed behind the plum tree that stood in the yard and for moments she was hidden from sight. They waited at the end of the corn rows, in the torment of July sun, and the thirst that dwelt on their tongues was abated a little because they knew the figure at the well drew the cool water from its dark basin of earth and poured it into the jug, spilling some of it because of the narrow mouth. In their minds they could see the traces of cool water flowing from the jug's mouth, spilling to the ground, and they wished the spill of water over themselves instead of the sultry streams of sweat that mapped tributaries over their dusty faces.

They thought at first that the figure had returned to the house. She was a long time out of sight again. Then they saw her emerge from where she had been crouched behind the well curb filling the jug from the unwieldy iron-bound bucket of cypress staves. At length she was on the road that ran along the eastern border of the field. They could hear in their minds the clug, clug of the water in the vessel slapping against the jug's sides with the sound of wavelets under the overhang at the creek's edge.

Meanwhile the field engulfed them. They waded in the green of the sea of corn, Danny to his shoulders, Jason to his armpits, the great Abner to a little above his middle that crowded the corn in the rows on either side of him. As he moved down the rows the corn blades that parted to permit his bulk flowed together again like the sea in the wake of a ship.

Since spring first began to stain the water their lives had been in the fields. For months after their arrival winter had walled them in, allowing Uncle Enid and Danny to become acquainted with the Preacher's household where they were welcomed as soon as the Preacher learned from Mary, who came from her sister's with them in the wagon, that the two were farmers and looking for a place to stay. Until their coming the strength of that farm had been far too small for its hundred acres. It had consisted of Abner as overseer and workhand, of Jason and the Preacher himself on the rare occasions when he was not attending one of his eight churches or visiting the sick, or meditating silence in the dark old living room in the northwest corner of the house where from the window he could lift up his eyes unto the hills, or behold the shepherdless sheep in the scraggy pasture on the far side of the creek. These three proved sadly unequal to the task of keeping the farm in full production and fully a third of the land lay fallow at the burgeoning of the year.

The Preacher, remembering the abundance the farm had poured into bin and loft and crib in the time of his father and in the time of his early husbandry, before he accepted the Call, was glad to add the four hands to the strength of the farm. But he stared first a long time at the hands of Danny, as if he wished them mature and unlocked from their shaping in the mold of youth.

In Danny's mind the green flood assuaged from the field, and he saw the bottom of this green sea as it had been on the wintry day of their arrival, brown and fallow earth matted with dead grasses and old weeds the winds of winter had entangled and rolled down. It was early March before it became apparent that the walls of winter were ready to fall away. Then the mysterious tints of spring came upon the far hills and the waters of the creek. When he looked at the delicate coloring of the water he could not decide whether its tints were actual or a reflection cast from the surrounding hills and banks that even in early March bore a ghost of color, a smoke of young green.

A phrase came in his mind when he first noted the change in the deadness of the winter landscape. "When Spring begins to stain." That was all the phrase. It came to no period of completed thought, was never finished, yet it had meaning. When spring begins to stain, he thought, and as if called forth by his thinking spring came like a seep, a stain of color upon the winter world. Looking out on the hills one day he saw them with their mantle of infant green about them, yet when he looked another day he could not be sure. It was as if there had been a greenish smoke that clung to the trees like one of August's least efficient fogs and the winds of March had blown it clear.

He enclosed the coming of spring in the phrase that lived in his mind. Now the phrase moved in his mind and he could see again, and feel again, even from the July cornfield, the conditions of spring.

As the sap rose in the trees and the first flowers began to open in the wayward places he felt inside himself a vigor that made him want to gambol with the young lambs in the spring pasture. Even the memory of this feeling quickened his movements as he hoed in the corn.

If the first seal of spring had been set with the signet of indefinite color on the hills, the March thaws were unmistakable evidence that winter was an old king too weak to maintain his kingdom, and they were glad to be released from his dominion. A fever of activity took them and they rode it through the busy days of preparing to plant. Each morning they rose at daybreak and went from the barn to the fields, Danny and Jason to clear with mattocks the sprouts and brier stools from the path of the plows, Abner and Uncle Enid driving the work animals, their chains clinking and jingling in a merry sound on the road. Abner drove the work mules, halloing and gesturing behind them, flinging first one and then the other of his mighty arms as if he meant to cast them from him. Uncle Enid drove his own mare to a one-horse turner the Preacher had found in disuse at the farm of one of his flock. (He found many things he needed thus, and his people gave and rubbed their hands together in a gesture of satisfaction because they felt honored by his taking.) All day long the plowers moved around and around and distance grew ribs behind them. Danny and Jason looked up now and then from their work and stood watching as the plowers inscribed a field, knitting with the brown threads of the furrows until each field was knit completely together into a brown shawl. When one field was finished they went without loitering to another and prepared it for the planting.

When the Preacher saw the land would be productive again, the last acre of it, he was happier than he had been in a long time and went back to the dark old living room and meditated silence. As soon as the planting was begun he left Uncle Enid in charge to manage as he saw fit, and the great Abner, relieved of the responsibility of management, worked with renewed vigor because his mind was as free as a child's.

The bearer of the water jug came along the road that ran to the east of the field. To the west of the field the creek ran. They could hear its voice conversing with the rocks that ruffled its flow at the rapids. In the deeps the creek flowed without energy or voice, reminding them of a lazy man that kept silence. They hoed with the creek at their backs, impatient for the bearer of cool water from the well. The water of the creek was too warm to stanch their thirst. As the figure came closer along the road they saw that it was Mary who brought the jug.

It was while planting that he had heard the sudden sound of crows. They cried *caw* several times in their rasping voices and then fled from the edge of the field with a great yammering and flapping of wings. He remembered that crying, as if they accused, with the same immediacy he remembered the change of Mary's figure that swelled still with the passing of time, and the bright flowing of his own blood, the dripping of his own blood upon the ground and over the golden flesh of Jason's arm as he held the wound. That had been after the planting, and he rubbed his fingers over the scar on his left wrist and saw the field where he now worked new to him and yet to be established in his experience by the mark of his foot upon it. Under Abner the fields of all the farm and the pasture had fallen into disrepair, like uninhabited houses. In the days after their coming the farm began to take on a new look. The pasture that had been as shaggy as the neglected mane of an old horse was sprouted in the lulls of fine weather that fell in February when it was good to escape the house. Even in blizzards they repaired the fences until the pasture was secure, like a house whose doors are proof against entry or egress. He and Jason had been set to trimming the hedges and the banks of the creek and when they were done the farm had the appearance of a man fresh from the barber. And because the farm was neat and prosperous looking a feeling of pride began to grow in them and they went gladly to work where they had gone unwillingly before. The work went forward smoothly, and when the time for planting came each thing was in its place. Those who came and went by the road that ran through the farm said that all went well at the Preacher's.

Slowly spring emerged from winter with its resurrections and lengthened, casting the shadow of its leaves toward summer, and their lives had been in the fields. Now it was July and the corn, running in straight rows from one border of the field to the other as if to preserve the air of well-keptness and order the whole farm wore, stood to his shoulders and in the woods the leaves hung full and finished from the boughs. Soon they would lay the corn by and the order of their lives would change. For months they had spent each waking hour at a necessary task. Fatigue sat upon their bones. Soon the strength and vigor that had flowed from them into the ground would be renewed in the good hours of liberty before the harvest demanded their energy again, completely, to the monklike exclusion of pleasures or desires.

He could see Jason hoeing in the row ahead of him. The dirt flowed about the corn roots in a little brown flood with each stroke of the hoe. As he looked at Jason's back that rippled with the motion of his hoeing and glistened from the sweat that gathered into a stream and flowed the course of his backbone into his trousers, he remembered him suddenly as they lay on the creek bank in a leisure hour when the corn had been twice cultivated and was knee high to a tall man.

They lay together on the creek bank and he said from a silence that had been a long time between them, feeding on the drowsy sense of well-being that flowed between and touched them on each side like the creek its banks, *I know what time of year it is.*

Jason had turned his head and looked at him and said, *Any fool knows what time of year it is. Any fool knows that.*

But I know what time of year it is in a different way.

What way, then?

It's the time of the high sun. It's what the Indians said.

Jason, saying nothing, let the term stand uncontradicted and together they stared at the sun riding in the very center of the cloudless sky.

From that moment summer dated in his mind. The days opened blue and unruffled like morning-glories, or storms stepped down from the hills with thunderous tread.

On a day they went out to the fields. The air was heavy and sultry and a few clouds lay lengthwise across the lower border of the sky. The rows of corn in that field ran east and west and the first light slanted from the long green blades of the corn. As they moved westward it rippled and fell from the rumps of the mules the plowers followed to the cultivators. Toward noon the sky was overcast, the wind blew faintly, scarcely stirring the still corn whose broad dark blades were spotted with light, as if part of them were in the shade and a part in the sun, yet there was no sun and by this sign they knew it would rain as certainly as if the drops were pattering already upon the blades.

But it is unthinkable to leave a cornfield until the rain begins. There exists always the possibility that the shower which seems imminent may expend itself in the hills, or pass high on the wind to another country. Plowers and hoers move back and forth along the rows, thinking with the unengaged parts of their minds what they will do with the respite granted by the shower which threatens.

So they remained in the field until the rain came in great shining drops that turned the corn a yet deeper green. He and Jason were allowed to ride the mules from the field. They rode with the backs of the mules between their knees aware of the music of the rain on the young corn blades, and of the coolness of it upon their hot flesh and of the steam rising in soft clouds from the backs of the mules; and of time to spend as they pleased, the gift of the shower.

He was hot and thirsty now, and the bearer made slow progress along the road at the east of the field.

Because the talisman of scar was in his sight he saw Jason again without looking at him and they were in the woods by the river. The shower had swept beyond to the northeast and all the fields were a mire from the waters of the rain. The afternoon was theirs, and they went from the house like young colts while Ezra looked after them, yet not uttering his whole vocabulary, while he questioned Mercidy with tugs at her skirt as she sat sewing on the porch.

"You cannot go," she said, and they heard the words before they were beyond the yard's edge.

That had been the time of the wound and his blood's flowing. The knife passed through the flesh of his wrist and there was only a stinging sensation; there was no pain to speak of but when he saw the blood begin to flow he was afraid. The knife passed through the flesh and it parted and lay open a moment like the mouth of one whose lips are drained of color. Then the blood began to flow. At first there were only small crimson globes that gathered at the bottom of the cut, and then he flexed his fingers and it was as if he had opened sluice gates to his heart. The blood leaped from the cut in a stream the size of a pencil.

He began to whimper. He held his arm out from his body, palm up, and stared at it as the blood flowed over his hand and dripped from his spread fingers, pattering like rain on a leaf that lay under the flow.

Even to his own ears the sound of his whimpering suggested the cry of a pup, and as the sound reached Jason he saw him look about him as if to discover a pup in the leaves at his feet. Seeing nothing Jason continued to whittle at a notch in a stick he held in his hand. When the notch was finished and the stick slipped again into its shell of chestnut bark it would serve as a whistle to mock the quail that called in the woods.

A ratchet of sound escaped his lips again and Jason looked and his eyes fastened upon the arm extending from his body and the blood that flowed from his fingers.

"Let's see," Jason said, "you've cut yourself."

Jason took the injured arm in his hand and the blood flowed over his own hand as he looked at the wound.

"That's bad," Jason said, and the fear that had been in him flowed into Jason at his touch and he was no longer afraid. But the blood spurted anew when he opened the wound, and Jason pressed it together again and held it, the pressure of his long fingers hurting the flesh.

He cried out against the hurt from Jason's fingers and tried to withdraw his arm from their grasp.

"Don't," Jason said. He stood holding the arm with his right hand and pressing the wound together with the fingers of his left. He saw Jason through a mist of pain, for the wound was beginning to throb and burn, as if a heated iron had touched the flesh of his wrist. When he saw his blood spurting scarlet over the golden flesh of Jason's arm a trembling set up in his body. It was not the trembling of fear. He did not know what it was.

"We have to go to the house," Jason said. As they walked the blood spurted afresh at each step. "You will bleed to death," Jason said then, but the shadow and shape of death did not approach with his words, and Jason removed his fingers from the wound and shifted his right hand so that it was above the wound with the thumb pressing against the vessel that rivered the blood. The blood ceased flowing then and they looked at each other and smiled. The bars were gone from Jason's eyes, washed away in the river of his blood, and now that the barriers were removed he saw the depth in them was limitless, like the distances which measure the sky.

As they made their way to the house he bore the twin wounds of the cut and the touch of Jason. Before they had gone far the sun that hung huge and red and perfectly round behind the gauze of clouds that streamed backward from the path of the shower fell against the far horizon and lay wrecked in a coign of the hills, a great bent coin diminished by half in its fall.

When they reached the house they avoided the front where the Preacher who would be stern and questioning likely sat, and entered the kitchen door. The old woman Mercidy was there when they entered. She looked up from the sewing in her lap and there was friendly greeting shining in her old eyes. She looked at them as if it were a great joy to see them, and then she saw that something was wrong and she threw her head back and peered from under her glasses.

"Mercy me!" she said when she saw the blood. She rose from the rocker, spilling her sewing about her feet, and the Idiot who was at her side clapped his hands together and cried, "Boodle, boodle, boodle!" as if he were celebrating some joyous occasion.

"Say the words," Jason said to his grandmother. "Say the words that will stop the blood."

She lifted her head and her eyes closed and her lips moved; she stood moving her lips in the shape of words and as he stood watching her he had a strange sensation of fear. The figure before him was like one in a nightmare who would warn him of some danger, yet could not manage speech.

"She's saying the words," Jason said, "she's saying the words that will stop the blood." Jason released his arm and the blood flowed less freely; it dribbled and ceased to flow altogether. He stared in wonder at the old woman.

"What are the words?" he said, and Jason answered him: "*I* don't know the words. If she told they wouldn't work any more."

He sat on the floor. He was weak and tired and he sat on the floor and looked at Jason. Their eyes locked and they stared at each other. Jason was smiling. His lips were curled a little at the corners. Jason stared into his eyes and continued to smile as he lifted his arm and took a handkerchief from his pocket and with slow, deliberate strokes began to wipe the blood from his right arm.

With that action of Jason's his memory shattered like glass and flew in slivers about his mind, so that he had no recollection of his wound's healing. He saw the field again where he hoed. In the shoulder-high corn he breathed deeply, seeking a cool breath of air for his lungs. It was hot between the rows. The sun hung a third over in the arc of the sky. The shadows leant toward noon.

But it was not noon. Noon was a time of rest. A time of lying in the shade. Now they hoed in the corn, Jason first, his hoe flying, the naked golden skin of his back rippled and bunched and reflected the light of the sun as the hoe rose and fell in his hands. Abner hoed at Jason's heels in the next row over. Sweat stained his old blue chambray shirt to newness. His great torso filled his shirt to bursting and ballooned over his belt that was completely hidden in a fold of his flesh. Now and then Abner took the tattered straw hat from his head and held it in one hand while he cupped the sweat from his face with the other, flinging it in a ponderous gesture to the ground. The ground drank the sweat as if it were thirsty.

He followed the other two at his own pace. And now Jason turned and looked backward at him while he rested his hoe on the ground. He opened his mouth and heaved his naked chest in exaggerated huffing. He smiled, the hard bright look of his eyes softening for a moment before Abner was at his heels, the threat of his hoe blade sharp and bright in the arc of a stroke. If it had not been for Abner Jason would have adjusted his pace to fit his own, but he would not be outdone by the great Abner. It was a matter of pride with him to keep ahead of the automaton that did not know the feeling of exhaustion in his mighty muscles.

Jason.

The sea of corn assuaged again and he stood in the road on the January day of their arrival at the Preacher's, with Mary in their wagon, and stared at Jason and the Idiot who came to see who was with their mother in a strange wagon. The Idiot clapped his hands together and smiled and said, "Boodle, boodle, boodle!" and he stood aghast at this greeting that was warm and without wit and terrifying because of the marriage of the disparate elements in the sweet, pure voice. He avoided the Idiot with his eyes, uncertain of how to look at him without betraying himself to folly before he saw how the people to whom this simple belonged accepted him. But to Jason he offered himself, the stranger at the gates, in the openness of his countenance, and was rejected. Jason had not smiled but stared at him coldly with his still, shut stare. Jason had stared at him coldly and then stood looking to one side while his mother lifted the Idiot in her arms and received in her neck his greeting that was the same as his good-bye and all his utterances between, "Boodle, boodle, boodle!"

In the interim since their coming in the wagon there had been much between them but the relationship remained fluid, a history of approach and withdrawal, and he was warmed or chilled as the climate shifted from temperate to glacial in the other's eyes. At times he was allowed to share the life of the

Preacher's eldest son as if they were brothers, but at other times he was cast out and again the stranger at the gates.

The others had come to slow assessment in his mind. The Preacher himself was a remote figure that moved with a cold dignity even among the simples of the farm where the others were warm and as vital as the livestock in the barnyard. There was a Biblical flavor to his speech and being that was one with the words of the prophets who lamented in Jericho. The Idiot dwelt shut from him forever in his whole vocabulary, the three nonsensical sounds, "Boodle, boodle, boodle!" Mary was a warm and beneficent presence but removed from him by her position as the Preacher's wife, and as the mother of Jason and Ezra. The old woman Mercidy sang in her cracked voice and the grandmother of his memory stirred sometimes the cocoon that had been her wrappings when she had lain on the board between two chairs.

But even when he was out of sight Jason postured always in a window of his mind.

A bird fluted in the unembellished silence and he looked over the field in the direction from which the birdsong came. A dozen rows away he saw his uncle where he moved through the corn rows behind the mare, remote as if he were completely shut away from the others. All day long he moved back and forth in huge silence. From where they were, Danny could see only his head and shoulders above the corn rows. It was as if a bust moved back and forth at the corn level. He moved now in the direction of the creek. Soon he would turn and move back in the opposite direction.

A breath of air swept over the field. The corn blades trembled and made a low rustling sound that gritted between the teeth. He lifted his face to the breeze and drank it thirstily through his nostrils. It was in his mind that the shadows were shortening toward noon.

The creek bank was to their faces again. The dark green of the corn rows abutted the lighter green of the growth of weeds at the creek bank. When they reached the end of their rows they looked at each other a moment and in silent agreement stood resting on their hoe handles, leaning, like the shadows, toward noon while they waited for Mary to come up to them with the water. At first they could not tell if it were she or Mercidy who came. The two alternated in the task of bringing water to the menfolk in the field. Each was glad of the task because it freed them momentarily from the prison of the house, and because the water was always gratefully received, in going to the field with the great earthen jug tugging at their arms they felt like bearers of good tidings.

When Mary reached them at last they drank from the mouth of the jug, each in his turn, and the weight of the water forced its flow down their throats to a sound of gurgling like that of a hidden brook. They let the water escape from their mouths and trickle over their chins and down their chests. The touch of the water cooled their flesh, and each handed the jug to the next drinker refreshed and ready to return to work in the sweltering field.

As they drank the Preacher was mysteriously among them. Eschewing the road he had come on a tour of inspection through the field. For a moment they wondered why he had not brought the jug. He stood among them, pleased with the prospects for a good harvest, and smiled upon them, the workers that had wrought in the field and been rewarded with the rank growth of the corn. He drank in his turn from the jug, last because he had not endured the labor nor the heat; and when he gave the jug again to Mary she lifted the empty vessel to her hip and went from the field.

As she returned toward the house they stood yet on the bank watching her go. She moved with her slow easy gait along the road. When she came to the point where a bluff lifted the road at the field's edge she was silhouetted against the sky. Her figure gathered to itself light from the sky behind it. They looked at her, Uncle Enid, come from his plowing, the Preacher, and all the others in unison, and they thought solemnly: All things burgeon in the summer weather. Mary was big with child. Her spreading figure filled the whole sky on their horizon with portents of birth.

2

JASON

The wind wave that had gone all across the field turned and came back and ended with a little shiver of motion in the grass that grew at the edge of the field where the corn ended. Jason lifted his hoe and let it fall with a regular motion and at each stroke the soft dirt flowed about the stalks of the corn. Abner hoed at his heels and he hurried faster than he would have ordinarily to keep ahead of Abner.

The creek ran the boundary of the field on its western border and it was stained a translucent green by the scum that clung to the stones and fluted out in continuous motion with the motion of the water. The muskrats that made their home in the bank of the creek stole forth in the night and gnawed the tender stalks of corn, and as they hoed Abner cursed them under his breath in a voice that rumbled from his chest like echoes from a cave. With each stalk cut he saw one ear less in the crib and as he hoed to the creek and saw the ears multiplied and the crib shrunk he cried upon the rodents maledictions and muttered curses. The other two strained their ears to hear the words and could not but feel the whorls of their ears seared by the imprecations the man had learned from his blood that had warred with enemies thieving from its sustenance since the foundation of the world.

Jason wetting his lips with his red tongue whistled against the wind the tune to the words he was following in his head, and for none to see the words:

> There was a lady and she lived near town
> And children she had three,
> She sent them away to the North Countree
> To learn their grammary

flowed in the mystery of his brain like the mournful sound of dove voices in a dark stand of pines. In his mind he had for accompaniment the sound of his grandmother's voice singing the words, for it was she who had taught him the song.

Abner, with the muskrats in his mind still, said, "I don't see how you can whistle among such waste."

"If I don't whistle will the corn grow again?" Jason said, and he stared at Abner with his still, shut stare. The words were changed in his head and Sweet Afton ran there; the stream of a boozer in Scotland whose tongue was a pipe his grandmother said flowed in his mind and blended with the sound of the creek without name that flowed on the boundary of the field at its own mysterious will, now calm, now turbulent.

When the song submerged in his mind he thought of the corn. One stalk grows with its leaves one way and the next stalk spreads its leaves in the opposite and the third parallel to the first, and so on forever. That is so the leaves can drink the sun. Abner was saying something about when he was a boy. He had not heard the first of what Abner was saying but he did not ask him to repeat the words; he waited for further words and then pieced out a meaning for the unheard phrases from sound and inference, and when he was through Abner was ahead again and his mind had to go like a race horse to catch up.

"Well, *he* had found a partridge nest," Abner was saying, "and I was a kid and wanted to find me one with the little speckled ones in it. I hunted in the rye while the others cradled and I found what I thought was an old partridge on the nest, but. . . ."

When he heard what Abner was saying Jason relaxed. He knew from a previous hearing that it was not a partridge that Abner had found, and he could see in his mind how Abner's small-boy hands hovered over the snake he thought was a nesting bird, and how the steel-taut body of the snake was moved by the faintest tremor before it was ready to strike. Then God, or whatever name he is known by, prodded the boy with insistent finger and he fell back suddenly and the snake struck wide, wasting the ambeer of its poison upon the ground.

He could see his mother, or his grandmother, he could not tell which, filling a jug with water at the well. When he thought of the water there was a great thirst that located on his tongue and he moved his tongue inside his mouth. His saliva was thickened and he spat and the saliva erupted white and cottony from between his lips. Abner's voice droned through the sound of the hoes, wandering back through the years of his life that had brought neither fortune nor famine but a plenty that had swelled his bulk to greatness and brought a complacency like that of a cow's to his spirit. He did not listen consciously to Abner. He had heard his tales and history before time and again, yet the repeating did not irk him. Abner's voice flowed as a deep counterpoint to the song that was still in his mind, bobbing in and out of consciousness like a chip riding the waves of a stream. When, with his mind far from the field, he cut a stalk of corn instead of the weed that grew by it Abner's voice lashed at him sharply, but soon Abner forgot to be angry and he forgot to care whether or not Abner was angry, and the wind wave ran over the corn again and died to a shiver in the broom that grew at the field's edge.

The song that had been submerged in his mind rose again.

There was a lady,

he thought as he saw the figure coming from the well, and the lady became his mother, for he saw as the figure approached that it was she who brought the water. She was yet small upon the road but he could see her figure distinctly. She carried the jug, sometimes at arm's length, sometimes on her hip leaning far over from her waist to balance the weight of the jug.

He turned and for a moment stared at Danny in the row behind him. Dirt clung to the fine face, and he was suddenly touched by the look of frowning concentration it wore. When the other looked up briefly from his hoeing he smiled at him and huffed to show that he shared with him the uncomfort of the heat. He repeated the other's name in his mind, Danny, Danny, Danny, and his mind was touched by impatience and it brought a frown between his eyebrows.

The blood upon his arm.

He saw Danny's blood coursing behind his flesh, the stream of it crimson and perfect in its unbroken conduits; and then he was in the woods with the other's blood warm upon his arm. The warmth of that blood had shaken him; he trembled as it touched his flesh. It was not revulsion that shook him. By his will the blood would have entered his own veins, and when Danny was occupied so that he did not see him he touched his tongue to the blood.

It tasted like salty water.

It tasted like brass.

It tasted like his own blood when his father had strapped him at the barn for negligence about the fence which allowed the cows to the corn. He was revisited for a moment by the emotion he had felt at the touch of Danny's blood and it aroused him delicately even now so that he hoed in a flurry of energy to drive the feeling from him. The song re-emerged in his mind and then sank again as he remembered the fading of Danny's face as they sat in the kitchen while he removed the drying blood from his arm. Because his hand was no longer about Danny's wrist the blood began to be repulsive and unclean and his flesh revolted against it as it had revolted against the fluid of his own body when he once polluted himself in a dream. As the handkerchief soaked up the blood from his arm the image of Danny who sat before him began to fade, and it faded while he scrubbed at the blood until Danny sat featureless before him and the blood was all gone from his arm.

His mother had arrived at last and he drank in his turn from the jug. They were all bound for moments in a solemn togetherness as sharers of the water. Because he smiled at what they had accomplished even his father, who had come on a tour of inspection, was not shut out. His sudden pleasure in their labor closed him within the circle and they stood in good companionship as his mother took the jug and went from the field.

Soon his father went farther into the field, walking slowly, casting his eyes from side to side and nodding his head as if what he saw was good. The others looked at each other in silent agreement and resumed their labor. He saw Danny's uncle, for it was only as the relative of Danny that Enid existed in his mind, move forward behind the plow. He had not slapped the mare with the lines nor shouted at her in a loud voice as Abner would have done. He clucked to her with the sound of a hidden cricket and they moved forward as if they two were of one body and mind.

As the hoes set up a clatter the song returned to his mind and commanded the sound of the hoes so that their even rhythm undulated to the tune of the song:

> There was a lady and she lived near town
> And children she had three,
> She sent them away to the North Countree. . . .

My mother's belly, he thought suddenly. He saw her in his

mind as she had gone from the field, the heavy water jug and the upward thrust of her belly destroying the balance of her form. He experienced a shock of revulsion along his nerves as he saw her against the sky. She is big like a cow, he thought, and he saw Ezra and himself and a shapeless mass that had no present identity bound to his mother by a cord that was like the cord of plasma binding mooncalves in a blood-stained, unspeakable sequence.

A memory shook him and he glanced briefly at Danny. Except for the faint curves of the muscles of his chest molding his shirt he was as flat as a board.

Danny in the woods, he thought. But he will not swell in his middle like my mother. He is not made that way. The memory lived in his mind and he saw Danny lying in unselfconscious nakedness by the creek bank where it flowed in the woods. They had been swimming in the pool that dammed behind a tree fallen across the stream. Danny had crawled from the water and lay with the shine of the water upon his skin, and he had turned suddenly and covered Danny's body with his own. The coolness of the water was between them like a chaste thought.

He was as naked as a rock. He is as bare as my hand yet. I made the motions against him because he did not know what a girl is for. I put my arms around him and held him tight against me. He put his hands against my shoulders and pushed.

He remembered when the water failed between them.

You are a fool, I said. He pushed against me like a girl would and I kissed his mouth. His lips were warm. He moved his lips under mine and I thought of something, I thought. . . .

But he will not swell in his middle like my mother.

He remembered Danny's eyes. They were like those of a person in flight, seeking refuge, and because of the impulse in himself he understood the other's panic behind the shaken barrier that was between them. When he saw Danny's eyes flickering in panic he rolled from him and sat up. He rested his hand upon his arm in a gesture of appeasement and when Danny had grown whole again under his touch they swam again in the water.

But my mother, he thought. She is big like a cow. The song emerged in his mind again:

And children she had three,
She sent them away. . . .

Sent them away, sent them away, he thought, and at that moment he began in the chill north of his spirit the term of exile from his mother which was his to endure until she should be delivered of the child that grew in her belly.

3

THE PREACHER

When the Preacher first observed the swelling of his wife's belly with child he went into the woods to meditate. This thing was not of his doing. This was an evil under the sun.

He had been reading in the living room. The sun outside was high and the light came through the windows and around his wife's form as she stood in the doorway looking out. He had been particularly aware of the light. I am the way, the truth and the light, he had been thinking. He was preparing in his mind his next Sunday's sermon. He had been thinking in the words of the Savior, and in terms of the Savior, but of himself also. *I* am the Way, the Truth and the Light. For was he not the road, and the word and the candle lighting sinners the way to salvation? How should they come to the true Way, knowing the everlasting Truth, or behold the great light of Salvation shining upon them in their outer Darkness except such as he exhorted with them and interceded for them at the throne of Grace?

Such were his thoughts as his wife stood in the door of the old living room where he meditated. Suddenly she unfolded her arms that had been lying folded across her stomach and he saw that her belly was beginning to protrude. His first thought was that she was becoming fat. How is a man who has not known his wife in two years to suspect that she is with child? He looked sharply at Mary as she stood in the doorway unaware of his scrutiny. Her features in general were no heavier than usual. Only her middle was swelling.

She turned then and came from the door, smiling absently at him as she went through the living room and entered the kitchen. He rose and went through the door she had just vacated. It occurred to him suddenly to see if he could discover what had held her attention as she had stood in the door. He could see the others where they worked in the field that lay fair to view from the little eminence the house commanded. Abner, his own son Jason and the boy Danny hoed in the corn. The man Enid, his workhand and overseer, plowed a dozen rows or so beyond the others. If he judged correctly from the angle at which she had held her head she had been looking at the man who followed the plow. Only his head and shoulders were visible above the corn.

He went through the barnyard and into the woods beyond. He found an open space and sat down on a stone. He began to make the gestures he used in the pulpit. Unconsciously he pounded his right fist into the flat of his left hand. Sometimes he gestured with his right hand, making motions like one sowing in a field.

A little my history, he thought, sowing it sterile upon the ground, flinging the fragments of memory like seed from his mind. He no longer desired his wife. He loved the sinner who sinned and the saint who repented. He yearned over the wayward with a delicate yearning that stirred him as love had.

But his wife.

He went back in his mind to the time when he had first known her.

A little my history.

For all his eloquence in the pulpit he was a reticent man, had been so in youth with the consequence that from the public places the other youths carried off the desirable girls while he was trying to screw up his courage to the point of asking her whom he chose for the pleasure of her company. He did not lack for beaux in his day, for he was of a substantial family and the homestead which was his to inherit, he being the only child, made him not a bad catch despite his diffidence in approaching girls. Yet the type of young woman he attracted did not much attract him. He would have liked to squire the more dashing, especially in the first years after he had successfully weathered the trials and withdrawals of adolescence. He heard accounts of strange permissions granted by some of the girls of the neighborhood. Yet at church and other public gatherings it was the more demure, the eminently respectable girl who found it convenient to put herself in his way, so that he could hardly avoid asking if he might have the pleasure of squiring her home. She, whatever face she wore or name she had, for there were many such in his experience before Mary, always accepted his company with expressions of surprised delight, as if that were not the very thing she had intended all the time.

A little my history, he thought, and he was back in the years of his courtships. They were dismal affairs. There was one thing on his mind and lacking courage to broach that subject with any girl he courted he found the time in the company of girls extremely tedious. From their talk he learned that other boys were furious when a member of their girl's family put in an appearance because a chaperon cramped their high, wide, and free style of courtship. But he was always happy if he could maneuver in such a way as to have the girl's father or brother, or even her mother, to talk to. Weather and crops were safe and comfortable subjects of conversation. Girls, he discovered, had only one topic of conversation. Let's talk about *us*, they always said, and what was there to say about us except the sweet, airy nothings he could never lay his tongue to, the sort of things one said to disguise the obvious intent behind cuddling?

Ah, a little my history.

As a result of his unhappy courtships he married the first girl that appealed to him strongly. He was twenty-four and had gone with Mary only twice when, pressed beyond endurance by the ache in his loins, he asked her to marry him. She said yes. She accepted him gladly, and not for the farm that would be his but for himself. She had been in love with him for many months, but in the manner of young girls hid the fact behind a front of indifference. He marveled that she had loved him in secret, had desired what he desired before he had looked at her twice.

He never ceased marveling at love until he had outworn it. The thought of love no longer stirred him like the brush of soft fingers against his skin. He no longer desired his wife, and the emotion he had felt each time on approaching her, an emotion strangely akin to fear, had seeped into the sink of time and now by night he lay unmoved by her side and slept.

In the first years after their marriage she had consumed him like wood in a flame. And then, after four years of marriage that had been a record of hunger and satiety, the incident occurred which changed the whole pattern of his life.

He had visited in another county and there he had seduced a girl that had been a virgin. That had been in the Indian summer of his manhood. His ardor for Mary was already beginning to wane and then when he saw the girl at the singing school where he visited with the teacher, he felt his manhood surge up within him and it was as if summer returned after frost and shone with its accustomed warmth upon a rebated landscape. In the clutch of the desire he felt for the beautiful stranger he found himself persuasive who had never been persuasive before, and he was able to have his will with the girl.

O a little my bitter history.

He felt even now the heavy hand of his transgression choking his spirit. As he thought of his transgression his hand caressed his face, for it seemed to him that it was bruised. It was bruised from the impact of a fist. He visualized the fist with perhaps a foot of the length of the arm behind it. It existed bodiless in black air, and it bruised his face, but whose was the shoulder that was the strength behind the fist?

After a moment his mind returned to the girl. After she had been delivered of his child she died. When he heard of her death the enormity of his act began to prey upon his mind, and there grew in him a revulsion against the act of love that wrecked his relationship with Mary. His desire was as great as ever but because his desire had brought death to the innocent it came to seem monstrous and he hated himself when he yielded to it. In the interval between exhaustion and sleep that followed on love his revulsion flowed out of himself and he was clean, but when God walked in that atmosphere and said, Where art thou, Adam? he answered from the edge of Eden, I did eat because the woman thou gavest me tempted me, and Mary lay at his side, the guilt of the forbidden fruit heavy within her.

Now, except for the memory of his own transgression which he carried with him always, he would speak to Mary immediately and tell her to take up her bed and walk. But even in his rage at discovering his household violated he was able to smile bitterly at the rightness of this retribution heaped upon him. It was an act of God and to be borne, and because he lacked the qualification for casting the first stone he would bear it. Besides there was his pride as he stood before the people. If he put away his own wife for sinning in his own house, how was he to stand before them and admonish them of their sins? He thought of a passage from the writings of Saint Paul: But I keep under my body, and bring it into subjection: lest that by any means, when I have preached to others, I myself should be a castaway. He was caught in a terrible dilemma and when he saw that he was he began to rock back and forth and make a psalm of his tribulation:

I speak and the ear of death is open to my words.

For I have become the grave of God.

In me is no life but the bones inherit the dust of the flesh and cry one to the other, what shall we do with our patrimony?

What shall I answer the bones?

Shall I say unto them: O ye dry bones take thy patrimony and cherish it as the miser gold and the thirsty water and the hungry bread.

Before it was shed from thee the flesh was a king in his kingdom and ruled with joy, the feet upon the mountains and the eyes in their sockets seeking to meet in the daytime the stare of God.

You have not inherited dust but the meal of a slow grinding.

Tears were water over the wheel.

Years were the grinding stones.

Men are proud in the flesh and their images are of stone, yet I will recount a history of dust.

It was a little in Eden alone.

Before day and before night the dust was.

The wind lifted the dust to try its first breath.

It became the companion of God.

For he stooped to the shell of his Image and blew into it the breath of life.

He exalted the dust. (Ye dry bones, cherish thy patrimony.)

Yet because the dust was wayward upon the earth it repented God that he had formed it in his image.

And he said to Noah: Come into the ark, and all thy household, for only in thee have I found righteousness in this generation.

But after the rains came and the waters were assuaged he made a covenant with the dust that he would no more destroy it from the earth. For it had breath without precept.

And he raised up Abraham and the fathers of Israel. Yet in the fullness of time the dust pitched its tents toward Sodom.

O weep, ye dry bones, for the weakness of the dust.

Yet above the city of lusts rose the uplands of Canaan. And the caves accepted the bones of the righteous in their burial places.

Into Egypt in bondage went the dust.

(The ear of death listens in the silence. The dry bones jostle one another, yet I will tell them a history of the dust.)

For to dwell in bondage is the beginning of freedom.

And the Red Sea bowed to the left and to the right and the dust passed over.

And it came to Sinai.

And the precepts of the fathers spoke on the stones of Moses.

Thou shalt may not be established without *thou shalt not.*

O dust, I am weary, weary. Do you bow to My Image? And when I speak is it the bawling of a calf for its father Aaron?

Between Moses and Christ the dust prophesied in Jericho and on Mount Hebron.

It was cast down before dogs at the walls of Jezreel.

The son of God spoke a word. I listened to his speaking and from the mountain I heard the word, and it was Blessed

Blessed

Blessed

Blessed

Blessed

Blessed

Blessed,

And Blessed,

And again Blessed.

O ye dry bones, blessed are the sons of men. They are kings in their kingdoms and rule with joy. Their feet are upon the mountains and their eyes are cast upwards to meet in the daytime the stare of God.

Incline your ear, O death,

For that the cup was not taken away in Gethsemane nor the cross from Calvary I am become the grave of God that he might not fall therein to corruption but rise, after the darkening of the sun and the earth's shaking, resurrected into time immortal.

Amen.

Because in his meditation he triumphed with the elders of

time he rose from the stone exalted, yet when he came into the presence of his wife again his exaltation flowed from him and it seemed that her belly swelled not only with child but because it was the receptacle into which drained his good impulses and his very humanity, leaving him a spare bundle of hatred and cloudy impulses toward revenge.

4

UNCLE ENID

So brave a battle is our love, Uncle Enid thought.

He had seen the figure at the well before any of the others, and he had recognized her immediately. Mary's figure was indistinct because of the distance, but his mind superimposed its picture of her over the actual vision and he could see plainly her face and even the cool color of her eyes from half a mile away.

When he turned the mare at the end of the field and plowed again toward the creek he could still see Mary as if she were before his eyes and not behind him, by now upon the road to the field. Because she approached he felt unsettled inside himself as he always did in her presence. The moment of their first and only consummation lived in his mind again and it ushered his blood faster through his heart.

That day on the journey when they had gone together into the woods and were beyond Danny's sight he had turned and laid his hands upon her arms, and his hands shook. When he touched her she did not shrink from him. She looked at him without fear or shrinking, and she said in a flat, calm voice,

"No."

"Yes," he said, and the tremor that was in his body shook in his voice.

"No," she said again and raised her hands to remove his own from her arms. When she touched his hands the warmth of her flesh burned him. She did not remove his hands immediately, she held them in her own and something like panic came into her eyes and her voice.

"No, no, no!" she said.

But it had been yes all the same. When he saw that she

would come with him from the wagon into the woods he had had no doubt of the outcome. It was as if two hungry people shared a meal, he thought, feeling within him again the same hunger he had felt when he had first known her and a sense of bafflement because the bars to its appeasement were many and seemingly insurmountable.

In the months since their arrival in the wagon he had come to understand that nothing is so hard to steal as love. They were afraid to look at each other openly lest Mercidy observe them with her sharp old eyes, or the boys drop suddenly their cloaks of innocence and stare at them with the insinuating gaze of the young. But their need for each other prospered inversely as they were unable to fulfill themselves. It was this need which held him to the fields and the Preacher's household. The power of her presence, he thought, the magnet of her face, and his original intention to move on from the Preacher's household at the coming of spring was forgotten before the possibility of a repetition of their love feast in the woods.

When he first saw that she was with child he was frantic for a time, thinking that their relationship had been exposed. When days passed and her condition went unremarked among the others he began to feel easy again. After all, circumstance was favorable to the concealment of their act of love which was beginning to bear fruit. Mercidy and Abner and the others when they began to notice would assume that the child that grew in Mary's belly belonged to the Preacher. He doubted at first that the Preacher himself had any doubt that the child was his own, until Mary disenchanted him:

He stood in the kitchen alone and Mary came from the living room where Mercidy was with the Idiot. The Preacher had gone at daybreak among his people and Abner and the two boys were on their way to the field. He caught her hand in his when she came near and she allowed him to hold it while she whispered in his ear.

"Go to the pasture," she said, "I will bring the cows."

"All right," he said and since he had the opportunity he began to pull her roughly to him.

"Stop," she said, "we can't. Mercidy is in the next room."

He released her and went by the barn and took a hammer and some nails and went to the pasture gap. After a while she followed, driving the cows before her.

Because they were alone together the day shone like a plate of silver. They dared not touch each other at the pasture bars, for they were in full view of the house and the field. He hammered at the fence as they talked. She made a gesture with her hands and brushed her dress down in a sweeping motion that outlined her form beneath it. She did not know how to say what she had come to say.

He smiled at her and said, "It will be a boy. I always wanted a boy of my own."

"Yes," she said. But she did not smile. A great misery was in her eyes.

"Mervin," she said, "the Preacher. . . ."

"Does he think it is his?" he said, and then because he wanted it not to be the Preacher's child he asked,

"Is it his?"

"No," she said. "No, it is not his."

He was suddenly unreasonably happy, as any man is, anticipating the birth of his child, for the moment forgetting their situation, but soon her mood penetrated his happiness and he stood looking at her gravely, questioning her gravely with his eyes.

"You had better go," she said at length.

"All right," he said and began to pocket the hammer.

"That's not what I mean," she said. "You must go away. Leave here."

"Do you want that?" he said.

"No," she said, and then, "I *want* you to stay, but it will bring trouble."

He did not know what to say, at that moment he knew only that he wished to remain near her.

"The Preacher knows the child is not his," she said after a while.

"How does he know?" he asked, and he wondered how indeed.

She began to blush, and he loved her the more because she did, but he persisted nevertheless.

"How?" he asked again.

When she managed to tell him it was that the Preacher had not known her in two years.

Suddenly his panic returned. That altered the matter altogether. That was a possibility so remote it never once occurred to him. He was angry with fate for allowing such an impossible quirk to exist in the situation.

"If he knows it will mean trouble anyway," he said.

"Yes," she said, "it will." She spoke in a dead, calm voice as if what she was saying concerned another person and not herself.

"If I go the trouble will remain, for you," he said.

"Yes."

"I won't go," he said shortly, "we'll face it together."

She could spare no more time at the pasture. She rose and went from him without another word. She walked heavily as she went.

He felt suddenly a revulsion against the whole affair and the urge to go and be free of it, nevertheless he would not leave her to face the Preacher's anger alone.

So life would not show condonation of their act by providing them with a camouflage? Let it betray them, then. They would find a way of their own, and because the way was their own, be utterly free. They would say like a disappointed borrower who has weathered his financial difficulty anyway: here I am and I owe no man. He thought then of the Preacher. Because Mary's condition was so patent no one could fail to remark it and the Preacher gave no sign of noticing, did not reproach them for their act, he thought of the Preacher with contempt. The Preacher was a figure of straw. He was alien even to the land he owned. He was a drone bee in an active hive. Because he was a figure of straw they would burn him from between them with the fire of their love. They would expel his foot from the land to which he was a stranger. They would destroy him from the hive. So brave a battle is our love, he thought.

Mary was halfway to the field, the water jug unbalancing her form as she came along the road.

When he had plowed the length of the field and turned again Danny pantomimed momentarily in a corner of his vision, and the sight of the boy lifted him to an eminence from which he saw his relationship with Mary in a different light. Instantly his regret at having fallen into the relationship was as deep and bitter as the physical need which bound them.

If she had not asked for a ride in the wagon, he thought, and he saw in his mind instead the dream figure that had preoccupied him in his own house in the days before the beginning of the journey. The form of Mary dissolved into the dream figure, and the dream figure and not she climbed into the wagon before the house like a four-eyed giant. The dream figure climbed into the wagon and sat between him and Danny. The figure was a girl younger than Mary, and fair, and after she had ridden between them her position and

Danny's were switched and Danny was between them without in any way destroying the contact that was between him and the dream figure. Danny rode between them and the circle which bound them was whole and invulnerable to breach or breaking. They came by the spot where they had stopped the wagon and he and Mary had gone into the woods, but now they did not stop for it was not necessary. The embodiment of that urge and that need was already between him and the dream figure.

When they were safely beyond the spot in the woods the dream faded and was diffused, and the road ran into a nimbus of light that made it impossible to identify the locality where it ended.

It did not end at the Preacher's house.

Except as it was modified to exclude actuality in the person of Mary he had had this dream before. In a manner he was betrayed by it. He had set forth from his own house with the intention of working its fulfillment, and his misfortune lay in that it was not the dream figure who climbed into the wagon. He should have been on the alert against mistaking the dream figure. He should have recognized at once that Mary was not she of the dream. She was not the foster mother for Danny he required of the dream figure for she was already married and had sons of her own. He had been betrayed by his hunger.

If she had not asked for a ride in the wagon, he thought.

The ground flowed backward beneath his eyes. It opened before the feet of the cultivator and flowed around them and closed again behind like four wakes behind a fleet of staggered ships. The dark, shapeless intrusions of his own feet in their stride alternated in his vision and to his right Abner and Jason and Danny were full in view when he lifted his head until he had overtaken and then passed them. Danny hoed behind Jason, and the figures were frozen in his mind like bas-relief carvings marbled in the postures of flight and pursuit.

He was again at the edge of the field where the road ran and Mary was only a little way from him. So brave a battle is our love, he thought, and then because the boy was still in his mind the bronze bravery failed from the theme and a cheapness was in its stead so that it made an ache in him like that which follows on the discovery of fraud.

He wished then that the world were one of simple goodness, that good and ill did not exist in tangles, and journeys did not abrupt into dead ends nor men exist always at odds but walked side by side like lambs to no slaughter. Then the image of Danny failed in his mind as he saw the figure of Mary bold against the sky, great like the sun in the west at evening proclaiming in a single brazen syllable the deathwardness of day.

5

MERCIDY

While Mary was gone with the water jug to the field Mercidy sat knitting by the kitchen door where she could look out along the road. She saw the other's back as she went, and her knitting lay idle in her lap while her eyes were on Mary. She counted on her fingers, touching them with her thumb from index to little and three back again, January, February, March, April, May, June, July. Then she took up her knitting again but after a moment the flying activity of her fingers lessened and her hands grew still in her lap gradually like boughs when the wind has passed.

In a voice that was thin and pure, except on the high notes when cracks ran through it like the lines in glaze on a piece of pottery, she began to sing:

> When summer hung upon the bough
> And field and wood were green
> O'Brady and his body-groom
> Were riding fast between.
>
> "What news, what news," O'Brady said,
> "What news bring you of home
> That in the three long years befell
> Since first I crossed the foam?"
>
> "Good news, good news," the servant said,
> "Good news of farm and field;
> Each fall of three you were away
> Full heavy was the yield.

"The mow is bursting with the hay,
The crib sags with the corn;
The wool would blanket all the poor
That from the sheep was shorn.

"The lean swine fatten on the grain,
The cattle on the grass;
And all your will that you made known
Servants have brought to pass."

"Good news you tell of field and farm,
Good news I'm glad to hear;
Now tell me of my house and hall
And of my Lady dear,

"For I had rather hear her well
And happy and at ease
Than have the yield of all the farms
Far-fenced in by the seas.

"And I had rather hear her fair
And sweet, as at farewells,
Than be the master of the hall
Wherein our sovereign dwells.

"For I had rather hear her true
And faithful as my bride
Than have a deed to all the world
That is so rich and wide."

"My mistress she is well, I ween,
And fairer than the sun;
My mistress takes her ease enough
While maids on errands run."

"And is she true?" O'Brady said,
"And is she true to me;
And is she true, my bonny groom,
As she did swear to be?"

"O she is true, and so I swear,
As ever lady was,
And she is true enough, master,
Though wonders come to pass."

"What wonders do you speak of now,
Of witch or conjurer?
And what have wonders one and all
To do with me and her?"

"The greatest wonders of the world,
The wildest wonders known;
The corn springs in my master's fields
Though not a seed was sown.

"The ewes grew great, or Easter fell,
When nights were long and cold
And lambed by ones and twos and threes
Though all the rams were sold.

"The mare that draws my master's plow
And makes the furrows run
Foaled the first quarter of the year
Though stallion there was none.

"The doe that haunts my master's woods
And pastures in the rye
Dropped then a little spotted fawn
Though not a buck was nigh.

"My master's Lady bore a son,
The fairest ever seen,
When he had twice-twelve-months been gone
And seas surged them between."

"Great wonders, these," O'Brady said
And prodded with the spur,
And silent they two rode the miles
That lay 'twixt him and her.

And when he entered at his door
The child was out of sight
And his fair Lady greeted him
With words that showed delight.

Said, "Come and rest you by my side."
Said, "Come and feast with me,
For it is three long weary years
Since first you crossed the sea!"

He said, "I'll sit down by your side
As soon as I am shown
That corn that springs up in the field
Though not a seed was sown."

Said, "I will feast beside my Love
When I come from the fold
To see the lambs the ewes have dropped
Though all the rams were sold."

Said, "I will drink my Lady's health
In wine when I have run
To see the colt the mare has foaled
Though stallion there was none."

Said, "I will kiss my Lady's lips
So pretty-primped to sigh
When I have found the fair fawn dropped
Though not a buck was nigh.

"And I will lie beside my Love
Nor turn till break of day
When I have kissed the son I sired
Three thousand miles away!"

The two they passed into the fields,
The corn grew shoulder high,
And though they digged about the roots
Seeds there were none to spy.

The two they left the field behind
And passed into the fold;
The young lambs gamboled in the sun
Though all the rams were sold.

The two they passed into the stall,
There shadowed from the sun
The colt was suckling at its dam
Though stallion there was none.

The two they passed into the woods
And looked both low and high,
And there they found the spotted fawn
Though not a buck was nigh.

The two they passed into the hall
And entered at a door,
And there they found the fair young son
Playing upon the floor.

O'Brady sat down by her side
As soon as he was shown
The corn that sprang up in the field
Though not a seed was sown.

O'Brady feasted with his Love
When they came from the fold
To see the lambs the ewes had dropped
Though all the rams were sold.

O'Brady drank his Lady's health
In wine when they had run
From looking on the young colt foaled
Though stallion there was none.

O'Brady kissed his Lady's lips
So pretty-primped to sigh
When they had found the fair fawn dropped
Though not a buck was nigh.

But when he saw the child at play
His heart was turned to stone
And from the door he came away
And left the child alone.

"I'll read your riddles now," he said,
"I'll riddle them a-right;
And when I have your riddles read
I'll lie with you all night.

"The corn was planted grain by grain
Nor sown abroad like rye—
And I have read you riddles one,
Now tell me if I lie!

"The rams went to the market place—
I read you riddles two,
And there were butchered in their strength
But each had known a ewe.

"The stallion champed above the mare,
I read you riddles three,
And then was auctioned at the Fair,
But big with foal was she.

"The buck had traffic with the doe,
I read you riddles four,
Before an arrow found his heart
And he was seen no more.

"And now but one remains to read
Before we take our rest:
My groom is father of the child
That suckled at your breast!"

They two slept each the other by
Like two to waken loath,
And rash and red there lay between
The sword that pierced them both.

When the song was done she was suddenly tired, and she
wondered for a moment what impulse had made her choose
that particular song from all those she knew and sang. She had
had when she began an unformulated feeling that the song
seemed to promise expression, but now when it was done she
was only tired, and the suspicion that had touched her mind so
lightly it was not clearly recognized had been dropped with
the stitches she saw had dropped from her knitting needle.

She sighed and gathered up the dropped stitches again.

6

MARY

Mary herself was numb and suspended in the vacuum that surrounds the coming to pass of a great event (and contained within her like a seed in the pod the unborn lay in the womb, its posture suggestive of an old man's resting. With head drawn to its knees it lay in its bath of water, stirring only now and then to achieve a more comfortable position. When the time was run it would issue forth, asking no odds of morals or philosophies. The concern now was to abide its time and it did so without impatience, contained and comfortable in its dark habitation).

PART IV

ALL LOSSES

UNCLE ENID

The darkness was in his mind, for it was certainly day. The Preacher had ridden forth more than two hours ago, and he did not visit in the night except to deliver, as it were, the good wishes of the Lord on the beginning of the last and lonely journey. And then only when a member of the family came and requested him.

Yes, it was day. The air was warm with the sun though the October sky had December's clear cast of light. It glittered on the lower hills that smoldered yet in the fiery siege of autumn, and fell from the shocks of corn yet unstacked in the fields. He saw the corn shocks, counting them in sections for stacking, yet he was half unaware of their very existence. The sound of the slap resounded in his mind still when he thought about it. It cracked like a faulty cartridge exploding in a gun.

Abner and Jason and Danny moved in his vision, carrying the shocks of corn. They moved in the lower section of the bottom, carrying the corn shocks on their backs like pack mules. They would put fifty shocks around a pole he had gone before them to place in the ground. Later, when several stacks had been carried up, they would all return and stack them bundle by bundle. He was ahead of them, counting the shocks so he could estimate the probable area from which they must be carried and place the pole as nearly in the center of this area as possible. Sometimes he counted upward of the required number and then lost count and had to do it all over again. The sound of the slap made a rage in his mind that blurred his thinking, that blurred even his sight.

The Preacher had ridden forth on his bay mare. He remem-

173

bered it clearly. He had heard him talking to Mercidy before he arose. Their voices came up to him through the floor of the attic and jarred him suddenly awake. He had lain listening because he could not avoid hearing unless he stopped his ears. That was before the time of the slap.

"I am going to Jarrards," the Preacher had said. "Mamie Jarrard is lying at the door of death. She needs the comfort of the Lord. At a time like that is when one needs the comfort of the Lord."

Mercidy answered him, the sound of her voice came to him outlined against silence. He had not heard her words.

"I'll be home by midday," the Preacher had said. "I'll come by the river road. One of the Lord's flock at Dewey's household is sick also. I'll stop by on my way home. Maybe I can bring some comfort to the afflicted." He remembered the harsh firm timber of his voice that went ill with his words.

The river road.

The shocks of corn spun in his vision, flying in golden clumps around and around, like swarming midges. He placed his hand over his eyes and when the swarm left his head he looked toward where the others worked in the field below him. With the shocks upon their backs their eyes were on the ground. He turned suddenly and made his way swiftly from the field, sounds like faulty cartridges exploding inside his brain.

When he had gone a little way along the river he entered the bushes on the point of a curve where he could watch the road from concealment and then enter the road when he saw the Preacher coming and walk to meet him as if he had been walking all the time. He could not come out of the bushes on any man.

2

MERCIDY

Mercidy sat with the child Joshua in her lap and hummed to him snatches of song from the grab bag of her memory. Now and then she turned her head to one side and listened for the sound of Mary within the house. When she heard her moving she was at peace with herself, but if not she had an unreasonable fear that the Preacher's blow had injured her seriously and she even had visions of her lying dead as a consequence of the blow. The Preacher from some impulse that exploded from his growing irritability had slapped his wife. Because there was no violence in her nature Mercidy had no understanding of violence, and she expected the consequence of its expression to be as terrible as she thought violence itself.

Now she heard Mary moving in the house and her mind was free to turn to the child. He had been only a month in the world and all the circumstances of his coming were fresh in her mind. His arrival had created dissension in the household. Not that he entered as a wedge into an undivided body. The members of the household were divided enough; indeed they were planetary in their reticences and withdrawals. And not that he arrived like a calf in a poor pasture. There was food for all and to spare. It was not that he came to a family too poor to clothe him. There was wool from the sheep for his sweaters and his booties. She herself had knitted them with pleasure, the wool thread feeding like a strand of time through her old gnarled fingers. When the time came she would weave him jeans as she had for all the others; presently there were things to be traded for calico and chambray at the store. Until the winter he would not need shoes.

The time of his coming was inauspicious.

She had begun to compute on her fingers some time before the child was born. She would pause in her knitting and sit for a long time looking into a corner without blinking her eyes. She would count on her fingers and nod, and then, as if questioning her findings, begin again, this time counting from little to index finger as she had counted from index to little before. Then she would take up her knitting again, but with a scowl on her face as if it were distasteful, though it was well known that knitting was her chief pleasure. She became so slow at finishing the garments that Mary began to think she would not finish them in time, that she herself would find it necessary to help and she dreaded the outcome of this for she was not good with the needles, and besides she feared to offend her mother-in-law.

But then Mercidy had had a happy thought. She had been much disturbed because the birth of the child promised to fall approximately nine months after Mary's visit to her sister and her return with the man and the boy in the wagon. She was highly suspicious of those circumstances until it occurred to her that Mary had been absent from her husband three weeks. What more natural than for a man to eat when he is hungry? she concluded, though she looked with extreme distaste upon men's sensual appetites, including her son's of whom she was proud because he stood before the people. No doubt then that the child was her son's and not an interloper to be sheltered by the vows of marriage which it violated. She was well pleased with her reasoning, and thereafter the garments began to be finished almost as soon as they were begun.

As Mary's time approached Mercidy began to prepare for the arrival of the child. When the garments were all in order and the midwife had been spoken for and alerted at intervals and the cradle from the attic refurbished she waited impatiently for the first cry of the infant. For with all her other activities she had been busy rearranging her crowded old heart to make room for the child. It was not as difficult as she had expected. It did not involve throwing out any of its former furnishings. At times she had felt that it was as full as it would hold, but there was room in it yet. She was too old to marvel much that there is always room in the heart. When the midwife laid the child in her arms and it curled its hands above its ugly little face she was impatient for the time when the hands would clutch out of affection and not from some residual instinct to cling or to push away, she was not certain which.

If anything marred her joy at the coming of the child it was the Preacher's attitude. When it was certain Mary's time was at hand she called the Preacher and told him to saddle the mare and ride for the midwife. The Preacher stood a moment looking into her eyes as if about to speak. Then he turned without speaking whatever was on his mind, clouding his eyes, and strode from the house. When she heard the sound of hoofs and looked out the window she saw the man Enid riding his own mare at a gallop, just entering the main road from the one that branched to the barn. She was surprised that it was he and not the Preacher riding for the midwife.

Afterward when the old priestess the midwife had performed the rites of birth and the child had been delivered coincident with the sacrifice of blood the Preacher was not to be found. Toward evening she found him in the living room reading the Bible. She was of a mind to give him a going-over with barbs in it but his face was grave and he seemed tired out, as if he had been fighting the wiles of the devil that, as he said, were so often thrown in his way. His face was so grave she was almost afraid to tell him of the birth of the child, but what man is not glad his child is born, and why, except for some great matter, is he not at hand when its first cry is sent out into the wide air of the world and not into the strictures of the womb? And if that is not possible why does he not rush at his first free moment to look on his child and comfort his wife, if it chance she is not asleep from exhaustion, for to bear a child is no small matter for all that it has been done from the beginning of the world? So she thought, and she had sharp words for her son, bred from his seeming neglect of his wife, but she had long ago learned when to hold her peace, so she said,

"The child is born already."

Still he did not speak, and she said as she turned to leave the room, "It is a boy. Are you not coming to look at him?" she could not keep sharpness out of her voice.

He followed her into the room where the child lay with his mother, who was asleep. Mercidy took the child from beside its mother and held it gently in her arms while she turned back the blanket from its persimmon-puckered face so that he could see it.

He stared gravely into the child's face for a long time but without speaking, and at length the child stirred and began to cry, and the old woman placed it back beside its mother and busied herself at some task in the room. The Preacher did not touch the child and she felt disappointed and puzzled besides and when Mary stirred in her sleep and he went from the room as if he feared she might waken and he would be forced to speak to her, she was glad to be out of the shadow of his presence.

Afterward he did not enter her room as long as Mary was confined, and Mercidy did all the work of running the house, and she labored in puzzlement because of the reception of the child by its father. His distant attitude revived in her mind the suspicion that the child was not his own. But when she was with the child she knew at heart that it did not now matter. She tended the mother faithfully and the child with pleasure because, as she thought, once the heart has received a tenant it does not know how to evict it again.

Yet all this wore at her temper. She was wroth with all the members of the household and quarreled at them impartially. Once when the man Enid was washing his face at the wash basin with a great rubbing and blowing as he always did, she told him henceforth to wash at the watering trough. He looked at her startled, but afterward he washed at the watering trough until she asked if he did not wash at all lately, having forgotten about forbidding him to wash at the bench.

As for Abner, she would hardly allow him in the house. Once he trailed manure over the floor because he had improperly cleaned his shoes after being at the barn. He discovered it himself and had opened his mouth to apologize when she discovered his trail leading through the kitchen. She had a broom in her hand because she was sweeping and she paused and looked at Abner with a slant look that did not waver. Her stare was more cutting than words and Abner became confused and hurried out of the house without a word. Except for meals and to sleep at night he did not enter the house for a long time afterward, preferring the barn and the company of the complacent cows and the ducks that resembled him in their walk, wobbling from side to side, as he did because of his great bulk.

To Jason the old woman Mercidy was less sharp because he helped her with the work of the house. She was a little afraid of him besides. She did not understand his tempers that were not expressed in the usual outward actions. When he was angry he seethed with contained fury, and yet there was no outward sign of his seething except in his eyes. She did not like to evoke the cyclonic glances that he directed at those who offended him.

She suspected that Jason resented the child, for it fell to his lot to wash the diapers in their worst states at the creek; then she boiled them to whiteness. It was unpleasant work, and she noticed that Jason handled them gingerly and the delicate rims of his nostrils quivered as they were assaulted by the soured scent of the diapers.

She took little notice of Danny. He was as constant to Jason as his shadow. He helped with the laundering and did not resent it if Jason gave him the worst ones to wash in the waters of the creek. As for the child, Danny himself had decided it was no concern of his. They were not of the same root. They were not linked by the ties of blood. He was free of any bondage except that imposed by his affections, free of entanglements save those thrown about him by love. He did not resent the child. While it was only a few days old he looked at the child with delight because it had the appeal of anything little, calf, pig, lamb, colt, it was all the same. The child in a way was like a toy also because it was a small model of something that existed on a larger scale in its natural state. It was a dwarf, or midget, he had seen one once, except it would grow up finally and lose its resemblance to a toy as dwarfs did not. He thought the child extremely ugly, as he was, but he knew that this was a state common to the newly-born, and one they did not always escape in growing up. Privately Danny considered the child a good potential, but until it should become old enough to engage in his own activities he preferred to have nothing to do with it beyond paying it the respect of his glance and smile when the grownups called it to his attention.

Of all the people in the house the one that did not provoke Mercidy or receive a sharp word or a stern look from her was the Idiot. He was the youngest except for the days-old child and hence the most lovable of all. As people advance up the ladder of age the chances of receiving a rebuff to the antennae of affection the heart sends out increase, so they take care and appear less lovable. She could not scold the Idiot whatever blundersome thing he did; her compassion for him was limitless to encompass his lack of intelligence. She was dissolved into pity and compassion and love when she looked at the Idiot.

And the Idiot was delighted with the child. When she allowed him into the room of his mother and held the child for him to see he sprang up and down while he clapped his hands and cried, "Boodle, boodle, boodle!"

It seemed to Mercidy that Mary the child's mother lay too willingly in her bed. She nursed the child when he was hungry and spoke the usual cooing nonsense to him, but otherwise she lay as if all that went on was nothing to her. She observed Mary looking at the child now and then with a quizzical expression as if she sought in his face the answer to a riddle that lay beyond her comprehension. If she noticed her husband's lack of attention she did not mention it and when Mercidy made mention of the Preacher's coldness toward the child she cast her a startled look and made her an evasive answer, as if she had not noticed.

"He has not been in the room twice," Mercidy said. "He has not touched him." There was condemnation of him in her voice for she could not conceive how any man could resist the urge to fondle his child, no matter if he has sired two already.

"He's doing the Lord's work," Mary said. "He will notice him in time." And Mercidy could not detect any concern in her voice.

Mary made as few demands upon her as possible, but she

was vexed when Mary seemed unmindful of the attentions of the neighbors, drawn to her by the birth of the child. Mary smiled when the visitors praised him and called him beautiful though he was not, but when they were gone again she turned from the light of the window and sighed and slept, as if she wanted never to do anything more but sleep.

Mercidy came at length to be troubled by a curious circumstance. The child reached the age of eight days without having a name given him, though it was usual to have a name ready for a child before it was born. As a matter of fact two names, so that one should not be at a loss no matter which sex the child turned out to be. When the neighbors would ask the child's name she would say, "Ah, he must have a special name, he is not named yet. We are thinking of the right name."

But it was not to pay respect to tradition and have an answer for the curious neighbors that she broached the subject of naming the child to the family. She had a name in mind that pleased her and she hoped that when she mentioned naming the child she would be asked for a suggestion. But she must not announce the name of her own choice before she had asked the others what they should name him.

On the eighth day when she found it convenient to be in Mary's room she said,

"It is time the child had a name. What name have you chosen?"

"Have you asked Mervin? He is good at naming. He can name for a reason."

She had no better luck with the others. Out of curiosity to hear what he would say she even asked Danny, but he only smiled and said he did not know how to name. She snorted, for she knew that if he had been asked to name a calf or a pup he would have done so immediately, or a duckling.

"A name is a name," Jason said when she asked him, casting her a shut look as if he were not interested.

She did not ask the man Enid because it was no concern of his, nor Abner.

When she asked the Preacher what name he had considered for the child it was plain that he had considered none. He frowned, looking up from his reading.

"A name, is it?" he said. He appeared to search his mind for a fitting name and she saw that anger began to collect in his eyes.

"We will call him Joshua," he said triumphantly. His whole frame was tense.

"Joshua?" she said, despairing of the name Manuel which had been the name of her dead husband.

"Yes, Joshua," he shouted at her, "because he was the son of Nun!" He laughed loudly at the pun which escaped her because she had not the particular knowledge necessary to fathom it. Later the drift of his meaning came to her, but then she was only puzzled and she stared at him a moment while he laughed and then began to back out of the room, impelled by his eyes. They were flooded by something that was close to madness, they shone and sparkled like pools of broken and splintered ice touched by the light of a cold moon.

3

UNCLE ENID

While he waited, hidden, two boys he did not recognize passed in the direction he had come, pushing and pulling at each other, the dust rising about them as their bare feet slapped slapped against the dusty earth. A horseman came in the other direction and he peered, tense, around the sprouts in which he hid. It was not the Preacher.

An hour passed slowly, eaten away in bits that fell soundlessly in time's stream like chunks of earth from an eroding headland into a river. Impatience and anger crowded behind his eyes, making a dimness there. He glanced at the sun. Through his anger it appeared round and dark as when seen through a smoked glass. An evil cast of light lay upon all he could see.

While he waited he witnessed again the scene in the kitchen. The scene was re-enacted in his mind with all the sharpness of detail of the original event:

The Preacher had slapped Mary. Without reason he had slapped her. Because her hand was on his arm, because she touched him to remove lint from his coat sleeve he thrust his face forward and said with sudden cold fury,

"Take your hands from me, woman. I'll not be defiled by a touch of your hands."

Mary had stood looking into his bitter eyes, gripped by such a paralysis the bird before the snake knows, her hand still upon his arm. As his right arm rose she swayed backward from the waist, her eyes round and dead she bent her body backward following the rise of his arm until it was higher than his head and back of the straining shoulder.

The sound as he slapped her cracked in the room like the report of a faulty cartridge.

Falling, she cried out once. She fell with her shoulder in the angle of floor and wall and lay silent, staring at the Preacher with dumb reproach, until Mercidy lifted her to her feet. Mercidy stood holding her against her old shrunken breast, her face turned from her son the Preacher who suddenly cast her a shamed, beseeching look.

When he saw his mother repudiated his act the Preacher turned abruptly and went from the house. When he had gone the others, as if suddenly released from intolerable tension, sprang from their positions, from the postures in which the Preacher's outburst had caught and froze them, and left the room. None of them had spoken a word.

During all the morning his anger against the Preacher grew.

At last he heard the feet of the mare drumming upon the road. He had memorized her gait from innumerable hearings as the Preacher came and went from the house. He rose and looked up the road. He saw the blaze in the mare's forehead flashing with the arrogant tossing of her head. He scurried a little back and entered the road. He was walking along with careless stride when he came up with the Preacher.

When they met the Preacher drew up on the reins suddenly and sat in the saddle looking at him with a cold stare.

"I thought you were in the field," the Preacher said. "What are you doing here?"

"The road's free," he said. He was surprised that the Preacher should question a free man of his right to be where he pleased. In agreeing to work for the Preacher he had surrendered up none of his privileges to act as a free man. "I thought I would take a walk. I've been working too hard lately," he said after a moment, and his voice had an edge of satire.

The Preacher snorted, couching his opinion of the latter part of the statement in a sound very like his mare would make. The loudness of the snort startled even himself. He had not meant to make it so forceful, yet after it was uttered he was pleased. He urged the mare forward. He had no time to waste standing in the middle of the road making nonsensical conversation with his hired hand.

"Wait," Uncle Enid said, laying his hand on the mare's reins. His hand remained holding the reins while the Preacher stared at him and he searched frantically in his mind for a decision he had neglected to make. In all the time he had spent waiting in the bushes he had not planned what he meant to do. He had an urge to thrash the Preacher within an inch of his life for slapping Mary. Yet if he did so he would have no alternative except to leave the Preacher's household, and Mary, behind. He was certain he could not persuade her to go with him.

The Preacher slapped the mare again with a twig he had in his hand, and she tensed to move forward but Uncle Enid's hand on the reins restrained her, nullified the power housed in the magnificent muscles bunched under the glossy skin. The mare rolled her eyes in fright, shifting her weight from shoulder to shoulder, her feet prancing without leaving the ground.

"Wait!" Uncle Enid said again, and he had it right in his mind. "Wait," he said, "and I'll tell you a parable." He heard again the slap, cracking in the air between him and the Preacher like the report of a faulty cartridge.

The Preacher waited. This was his enemy. This was the man who had defiled his household. This was the man he hated with his whole soul, and yet he could not acknowledge this man's sin to the world, nor the manner of it, and keep his pride as he stood before the people. It had long been in his mind to send him away, and the boy with him, but he postponed this action, first for fear his wife might go with them and shame him still in the eyes of the people, and secondly because—who knows these things?—the man might by some mischance come upon the fate he desired for him. If he remained and let him think about it carefully he might.

"What is this parable?" the Preacher said.

"You understand parables, don't you?" Uncle Enid said tauntingly, "you being a preacher."

"The parables of the Lord," the Preacher said, "let us hear this parable."

"This is not one of the Lord's parables," he said.

"Let us hear it," the Preacher said. He made an impatient movement in the saddle. The mare stood poised, watchful, the whites of her eyes showing.

"Once," Uncle Enid began, "there was a man lived in a far country, they always live in a far country, don't they? . . . and this man took unto him a wife and lived with her. This man and this woman lived on a farm, a hundred acres. They lived in that country and were happy together for the space of four years, for they loved each other with their souls and their bodies both, as they were supposed to do. After a time a son was born to them and they called his name. . . ."

He broke off, looking closely at the Preacher. He was using all his skill in making the parable sound like a real parable and he was slightly proud of the sound of it rolling from his lips.

"What does it matter what they called him?" he said, looking closely at the Preacher again. The Preacher stared back ·at him, his face still, the eyes in it cold and watchful. I should have told him the name, Uncle Enid thought, but he went on.

"The son was born and for four years they were happy together, but before the second son was born the man visited in another country. He was gone four days and while he was gone he was visited by the Spirit." The corners of his lips drew away from his teeth so that he looked a little like a snarling dog. The Preacher's head snapped back and then came forward, as if he had slapped him. "And the Spirit spoke to the man, and when he returned to his own country he was no longer content to farm the land but took up another profession."

The Preacher's face remained rigid. His hands were tense on the mare's reins, the knuckles showing white under the strain of his clutch. "Go on," he said, when Uncle Enid paused.

"When he took up the other profession," Uncle Enid went on, "he became a eunuch."

A flicker of motion ran through the Preacher's body. "I'll not . . ." he said.

"Or was he already castrated?" the other said, interrupting, smiling at the Preacher.

"It's your parable," the Preacher said in a terrible voice and settled himself in the saddle.

"It chanced," Uncle Enid went on, "that the wife of this man made a journey in the twelfth year after her second son was born. And on this journey she met another man and lay with him, because her husband was a eunuch, and conceived a child by this man, and the child was born."

His voice took on a strange timber. There was a strain of pride in it because he had fathered the child, and a strain of love for the bearer of the child, and a strain of contempt for the man to whom he confessed he had lain with his wife in the guise of a parable. All of this was in his voice.

He admits it, the Preacher thought. He has the gall to fling it in my face. If he should happen to an accident . . . but Uncle Enid was continuing.

"The man knew the child was not his own, knew it as soon

as his wife's belly began to swell, yet he was prideful and
would not admit it to the world because of his pride. He hated
the woman and at last he injured her. He slapped her against
the wall no later than this morning," he said, bringing the
parable to focus. As he spoke he heard again the sharp crack
of the Preacher's palm against Mary's cheek. "The second
man," he continued, "because he was a man and not a eunuch
was angry with the first man and thought to punish him
severely. But he changed his mind."

"I'll not . . ." the Preacher said.

"Wait," Uncle Enid said, "this is the beautiful part of the
parable. Parables must have morals, mustn't they?" He stared
at the Preacher. "He changed his mind because the first man
considered, and because the second man and the woman loved
each other he decided to go away and leave them in peace.
He decided to go away and never be seen by them again." His
voice was taut, cold and threatening. He waited for the
Preacher to react, to assent to the suggestion that was implicit
in the conclusion of the parable. He no longer heard the sound
that cracked like the report of a faulty cartridge. He had
acted. It now remained for the Preacher to act, to say whether
or not he would go and leave them together. If the Preacher
should not decide to go. If the Preacher. . . .

The Preacher lifted his hand as if to strike a blow with it.
His face was livid. His breath came painfully through dis-
tended nostrils, the sound of his breathing was clearly audible,
loud, irregular, like the breathing of a goaded bull.

They stared at each other in silence. And suddenly a muscle
in the Preacher's face began to twitch. The pulpy flesh over
his cheekbone began to twitch. It danced like a leaf in the
wind. He touched his cheek with his hand but the twitching
continued. Uncle Enid stared at him, his mouth hanging agape
like an idiot's. The pupils of his eyes contracted and expanded

as if from an effort he made to remember something tenuous
and almost lost beyond recall in the maze of his mind. And
before him suddenly there was the image of the woods at
night, and the moonlight streaming into a little natural bower.

"Merciful God!" he shouted as he remembered.

A flash of bewilderment passed over the Preacher's face.

"O Merciful God!" the other shouted at the top of his
voice, and he began to laugh, loud, gasping bursts of laughter,
punctuated between with sobs, as of a man who tries to keep
from crying out against a deadly hurt. His hands began to
tremble and shook the mare's reins and she arched herself
away from him, almost dislodging the Preacher from the saddle.

"Daisy," Uncle Enid whispered, staring intently into the
Preacher's face. "Daisy," he whispered again, his voice rising,
fanning the word out like a spreading fan.

The Preacher gave a start. The shoulder behind the disbodied fist that had been in his mind when he meditated in the
woods materialized. It belonged to the man before him. His
body stiffened and then relaxed as if he had come unex-
pectedly to the brink of a precipice, yet had caught his step
before he was carried over the edge. His body remembered.
There was a rising sensation in the region of his middle and
it sent a wave of sickness over him. His mind revolted against
the sensual interlude in the little bower by the road's edge.
He put thoughts of it from his mind lest they show in his
face. He made his face empty and looked at the man below
him. He said nothing.

Uncle Enid stared at the Preacher with narrow eyes, thinking: I must be careful about a thing like this. He began to
count and the words from his own parable based on facts he
had gleaned from Mary came back to him. *And before the
second son was born the man visited in another country.*

That would have been about the time of the stranger in the roadside bower.

"Don't you remember?" he said to the Preacher, almost pleading. "You couldn't forget a thing like that." The twitching cheek, he was thinking.

Fear gripped the Preacher's heart. He must not in any case acknowledge that long-ago sin to the man before him. To do so would be fatal; yet he could not flatly deny it. He lied so badly it was the same as telling the truth. If he could evade. . . .

"I'm a minister," he said, "I'm. . . ."

"Don't you remember?" Uncle Enid persisted. But he had already accepted the Preacher as the man running, running from the roadside bower. His mind had performed its arithmetic. It had recalled the vow he had made when he was come to majority and his pride was cut down by the disgrace of his sister.

"I'll refresh your memory," he said. "The girl at the Glade. The one who died after the child was born. You heard about that, didn't you? It was like a little fox and you made a cage for it in your breast. When you saw her face in the dark of the night didn't the fox begin to gnaw? Didn't it?" he said.

The Preacher sat silent on the fidgeting mare.

"Was that when you heard the Call?" Uncle Enid said. "Did you think you would make up for what you did to her by blabbering about the Lord?"

"I'm a minister," the Preacher said in a hurt voice because his integrity had been impugned.

"Hiding under God's coattail," Uncle Enid went on. Dimly he felt the trembling of the mare under his hand that lay against her neck, the reins in its clutch.

"Acknowledge it," he said in a dangerous voice, sawing the air with his free hand. Then his voice failed and his lips worked in silence. He moved his lips as if speaking, then he stopped for a moment to gather himself, and he said it, making the admission, "Acknowledge that you are Danny's father." The words as he spoke them had a bitter flavor, and suddenly he hated the Preacher more than he had known it was possible to hate. He had hated the stranger when he found him with Daisy. He had hated the Preacher when he slapped Mary in the kitchen. For moments now he had hated both in the person of the Preacher. But as Danny's father he hated him beyond redemption or endurance. He hated him because he loved Danny. He hated him because the fact of his fatherhood of Danny robbed him of the boy he had brought up and loved as his own son.

"If you touch him I'll kill you," he said irrelevantly, thinking of Danny. A lament for Danny began in his heart. The tears fell in his heart and his voice changed.

"I'll make you acknowledge him," he said. "I'll make you get down on your knees before Mary and Mercidy and say about Danny this is my bastard son. I'll make you give them the details of how it came about. If you touch him I'll kill you. You'll say this is my bastard son. I got him on a good girl twelve years ago. She died. If you touch him, I say, if. . . ."

He began to babble incoherently. His lips flapped together and spittle flew from them in a fine spray. He was shaking like a man with a chill. The trembling in his arm communicated itself to the mare's neck and she flashed the whites of her eyes, semaphoring fear in a lost code. She stood poised, ready to plunge forward.

Lost, thought the Preacher, lost.

He still sat in the saddle, half turned toward Uncle Enid, his right foot was free of the stirrup, his knee drawn up and clamped against the mare's side, his right hand gripping the reins over the mare's arching neck. His left foot was in the stirrup.

They stared at each other in stupendous silence. The twitching in the Preacher's face had ceased. His face had contorted to stone and not a muscle in it moved. Even his eyes were frozen in a look of hatred and loathing for the man who stood on the ground and returned his stare out of eyes that belonged in a beast's head.

Lost, thought the Preacher, lost. "Joshua," he hissed at the face below him. It was his argument, his answer, and on a sudden impulse he spat into the face below him.

The muscles in Uncle Enid's face froze and relaxed and rearranged themselves. It was the face of a dead man that was lifted toward the Preacher. Two large tears gathered and rolled from the set eyes. They were the tears the fist of rage squeezed from the stone of his brain. He lifted his hand and the stick he had used as a walking stick as he came along the road was suddenly in his hand, snatched from where he had stuck it in the ground. The stick flew half through the arc of a blow.

The mare ran. In terror she sprang forward suddenly with incredible speed. The Preacher was thrown from the saddle. His left foot turned in the stirrup and caught there. His neck was broken on the second leap. The flesh of his face and his blood and strands of his hair marked the stones in the path of the mare's going.

Uncle Enid collapsed in the road. He sat in the road trying to shut from his eyes the image of the man flying from the mare's side as she ran.

He was afraid.

The blow he had aimed at the Preacher had gone far wide as the mare plunged forward. The mare was guilty of the death of the Preacher. Yet he was afraid. He looked up and down the road to see if there had been witnesses to his quarrel with the Preacher. No one was on the road. He peered into the woods on the side of the road. No one was there, at least no one he could see. He surveyed the river that ran parallel to the road. No fisherman cast or angled from its banks. He looked overhead.

There was only the sun and a cloud or two and a hawk wheeling, far away, over the hill that marked the horizon.

He arose after a while to make his way by a circuitous route through the woods to the field. On his return there he found the others had not missed him. He resumed his work, and all the cells of his body listened for the approach of a messenger from the direction of the house bringing tidings of the Preacher's death.

Before they had finished stacking the tops the messenger came.

4

The mare's terror carried her forward along the road that ran by the river, past fields and houses, and led at length by the Preacher's house and into the country beyond. The weight that swung from the saddle stirrup increased her terror. Now and then in swinging it struck her legs with such force it almost tripped her. When this happened she drew up so suddenly she squatted on her hocks in the road, and then neighing in such a voice it shook the countryside she struggled to her feet and lunged forward with greater speed than before. With wild eyes and the suds of foam flying from her mouth that was held wide to allow the air to her laboring lungs she raced, the source of the terror she would escape flying like a bundle of rags at her side.

The children of Joab, the tall farmer who was a member of the flock at Confidence, one of the Preacher's small churches that stood a mile or so from Joab's house, deeper among the hills, played in the barnyard. There were four of them and they slid from the strawstack in the order of their ages, the oldest first, and when they were all down they climbed the stack once more. The barnyard lay at the road's side with an open meadow beyond it. The barn itself was lotted and it was in the center of this lot the strawstack stood, its base fenced from the cattle.

Here the children of Joab played when they heard the drumming of hoofs upon the road.

"Somebody's coming," one of them said, and the four, having reached the top of the stack, stood to have a good view of the traveler when he came first in sight. From there they had a long view of the road and they were eager to see who came since few travelers passed their place because nothing lay beyond it in one direction but the hills where there were a few

poor houses and a little church. In the other direction was
the Preacher's place and beyond the world, but the drumming
hoofs sounded from the direction of the hills and they were
curious to see whether it was a neighbor who rode at such a
hurried pace as the hoofs announced, or a stranger who had
come into the hills from another direction and was in a hurry
to flee them again.

"I'll bet it's Old Jack," the second of Joab's children said,
naming a crotchety neighbor who lived by himself not far
away.

"Nix," said the first, "it's not Old Jack." She wished it to be
a stranger carrying with him a breath of the great world beyond. "I know it's not Old Jack. His horse can't run that fast."
The others had a vision of Old Jack's stack of horse bones
and knew that it was so.

"Let's speak when he comes by," said the second. "Let's
stand here and all speak to him when he goes by."

"I'll bet it's somebody riding for the doctor," the third of
Joab's children said. "He's in a powerful hurry. Listen to
him run!"

The fourth child stood looking in the direction of the
sound, so it was he who was first to see the mare as she came
in sight. When he saw her he made a small sound in his throat
that was half glee because somebody came, and half puzzlement because no one sat in the saddle. When the mare was
nearer they saw something hanging from the stirrup and it
bounced up and down with uneven strokes against the ground.

"It looks like *somebody!*" the oldest of Joab's children cried,
and her voice lifted in a long shriek and died in the high reg-
isters of a bat's cry.

One of Joab's horses heard the sound of hoofs and neighed
in his stall, and the mare, hearing one of her kind, turned
abruptly from the road and stood at the barn gate, heaving

her sides. The thing that hung from the stirrup rolled a little
and settled to rest with a grotesque jointed movement. The
children saw that it was certainly a man who hung from the
saddle stirrup and when they saw the broken and bloody face
they dropped from the stack as suddenly as if a trap door had
opened under them and ran, screaming, toward their house.

Because he could make no sense from the incoherent voices
of his children trying to tell him a dread thing, Joab himself
went to the barn. He recognized the Preacher's mare at once,
and he saw what hung from her saddle and began to approach
her, speaking in the coaxing voice of a man long used to handl-
ing horses, but she began to shy away from him slowly, drag-
ging her burden with her.

He knew sudden enmity between himself and the brute
and lunged for the bridle reins, but the mare avoided him
and began to run, making a flying circle of the little meadow
beyond the barn. When he saw the mare, avoiding him, meant
to stay, drawing he knew not what comfort from the near
presence of her own kind, he went swiftly to the house and
brought forth his shotgun. The mare went by him again in
her circle of the meadow, and sighting along the barrel of the
gun he saw the look of terror and appeal in the mare's eyes.
But he hardened his heart, knowing he could not spare her,
and pulled the trigger.

The mare fell. The weight of her body, careening in a turn,
carried it to the ground away from the man hanging from the
stirrup. The suddenness of her fall jerked the Preacher's body
so that it was air-borne a moment and then struck her side
with a sudden dull thud. For a moment Joab turned his eyes
away and struggled to avoid the sickness that made a knot in
his throat.

He set the gun down carefully, knowing a brush of pleasure
at the mare's fall because it was a sort of victory of his kind

over her kind, then he carried the body of the Preacher and laid it on the edge of his porch. When he had done this he bowed his head a moment and stood with his hand to his face, not looking at the Preacher; then leaving the body ringed by the frightened faces of his children and his wife he started reluctantly in the direction of the Preacher's house.

5

MARY

At Confidence they buried him. Mary sat with her hands folded solemnly in her lap. Mercidy and Ezra sat on her right and Jason, with his public face on, sat on her left, and so she was enclosed in the circle of her family, except for the infant Joshua whom a woman of the wake had taken to hold. She longed to turn her head and seek him out with her eyes, closing the broken circuit, yet she looked straight before her and gave part of her mind, as much of it as she could command, to the words of the officiating minister.

"Dearly beloveds," he said, and the weight of the importance of the occasion freighted his voice and it slipped from his control and strained to silence. He began again. "Dearly beloveds," he said, his voice under control now, deep and firm and resonant, "we meet together today on a sad occasion. This our brother in the Lord has gone to his long home."

Her eyes were upon the box. Joab the farmer and his neighbors had fashioned it from walnut boards that came from Joab's loft, boards saved for such a need, his own or his neighbors', for in his eyes they were equal. They had covered it with a black cloth of a velvety texture. The handles were of a silver color and came from the hardware. A small square plate engraved with the word *father* adorned the lid in a position near the heart. It was of the proper color, for death is a dark thing.

While the minister recounted the Preacher's virtues upon the earth Mary was thinking of Joab, for Joab was involved in all the arrangements for the Preacher's burial, and in her mind he was involved in the death itself, not as in any manner contributing to it, but when she thought of one she thought of the other. Now Joab's hands existed in her mind. She saw them for a moment holding the plane that smoothed the boards for the coffin. They nested there in curls of wood from the plane's tongue, and then she saw them, large and bony, holding his hat and turning it with anguish as he stood at her door and told her of the Preacher's death.

"And his face is ruined," he had said, concluding his recital with this news. He looked from her and said reluctantly, as if he liked less to deliver this piece of information than news of the death itself, "His face is ruined."

That had been in the middle of the afternoon. Because only the two women were at the house Joab went further to the field and told the menfolk who came when he shouted from the field's edge with the reluctance of men interrupted at their work, until they learned why he called them.

They came, all of them except the man Enid who stayed to do the chores, with Joab to his house in the wagon. On the way she felt only a numbness that extended to all parts of her body. Joab had said the Preacher was dead, and she believed him, yet in her mind he was not dead until they came to Joab's house and she saw him lying on the edge of the porch ringed by the vigil of the woman and the frightened children.

Then he was dead.

They placed the body of the Preacher on a mattress in the wagon bed and began the drive to their own house. Mercidy sat with Ezra by Abner on the seat and she sat in one corner of the wagon at the Preacher's head and Jason in the other. As they drove she cried softly to herself, trying to number the wounds in his body, the gashes cut in the ugly purpling flesh, and with each one counted her grief increased. Jason sat stiffly in his corner, staring neither to the left nor right. He sat with a solemn face and did not weep nor speak a single word. Ezra was quiet on the wagon seat between the others as long as he was able to contain himself, and then he cried out gleefully, clapping his hands together, "Boodle, boodle, boodle!" These words she considered as effective to speak of death as any others.

On their way they passed houses that squatted on their little eminences like chickens at roost. At some of these children played in the yards, and their young voices came to them in the wagon, clear and boisterous and light, and the wagon seemed to run lightly as if to bear its burden in stealth beyond the affront of those innocent sounds. Evening was upon them before they reached their own house, and looking across a field she saw a lean black bitch foraging near the road. The dog stared at them with beady little eyes, and when they were past continued to search the ground, oblivious of the burden they carried in the wagon.

Word of the Preacher's death had spread over the countryside, and when they reached their door there were hands to lift the body from the wagon and prepare it for burial; hands to touch them in silence, seeking to impart comfort by their living touch.

If there was no comfort to be had, yet the night of his wake was somehow endured, the dark festival of tears and grief that is older in the world than the festivals of joy and song.

In the morning Joab, tall above others in his body and in his strength, went soon after daybreak and harnessed his bay mules that were strongest of all those tethered at the Preacher's barn. He hitched them to his wagon that would run smoothly and without clucking in its hubs because it was new, and drove it to the road before the house.

The early morning sun shone with an Easter brightness, and cast his shadow tall before him as Joab gave his lines to another to hold and went again to the house. He stood in the door a moment, his presence a signal to the others that the time for departure had come, and they all gathered about the man in the shroud. They stood looking upon the outlines of the face hidden beneath the cloth and to a second depth beneath the folds of the tissue of death.

They took leave of him in his own house, and they placed him in the box and began the journey, all proud in their hearts that Joab could give him respectable carriage to his long home.

So they transported him to Confidence.

When the words of the minister penetrated Mary's mind again he was reading: *For as in Adam all die, even so in Christ shall all be made alive. But every man in his order: Christ the firstfruits; afterward they that are Christ's at his coming.* The voice continued and she sought the strength that was in those of her own by her side. She had not yet yielded to tears and to escape them her mind clutched at thoughts of her family before the words of the minister again claimed her attention.

Then cometh the end, the minister read, and her mind took up his words. Then cometh the end, her mind repeated, but before the end could be accomplished there were two necessities: The first was to forgive the Preacher for his aggression against her when he slapped her against the wall. This she did and she saw that it was a gratuitous thing to do. The second necessity was to expiate her sin against the Preacher with the man Enid. This was a more difficult matter, it was not altogether accomplished in exchange for her forgiveness of the Preacher, for the two matters were not of an equality, so that one would cancel out the other.

The impulse to seek out the infant Joshua was still in her mind and she turned her head to seek out his face. When she did this she looked directly into the face of the man Enid who sat on the bench behind her. For a moment she did not recognize him. She stared into his careful eyes, and then a sense of shame threaded her feelings, and she saw at once that she must send this man from her. She looked at him a moment more, but in repudiation, before she sought and found the infant Joshua in the arms of the woman who had taken him to hold.

With the decision to send the man with whom she had sinned from her household as the first act required for the expiation of her sin, nothing stood in the way of her grief for the Preacher, and she yielded to it.

O death, where is thy sting? O grave, where is thy victory? the minister intoned, and she cried without uttering a sound: In my heart, and the tears came scalding from her eyes and she was cleansed by their flow.

Ashes to ashes, dust to dust, the minister declared. And they buried him.

6

MARY

The Preacher had been many days now a tenant in a narrow house in a timeless country. Whatever she was doing Mary remembered his commitment to that habitation, and strangely he was hers there as he had never been in life. She saw that the relationship of two people is dependent upon unpredictable contingencies, and for his part he was beyond these so her own attitude became static; their relationship rested now beyond contingency or threat, it was set and perfect, and she loved the ruined face as she had not loved it whole. She saw that if she had been unfaithful to him living she would be faithful to him dead forever.

Meanwhile the partner in her sin against the Preacher had vanished in the night, leaving the boy and his mare behind him. She was angered because he had gone of his own volition and thus robbed her of expiating her sin to the extent of sending him away. Yet her mind could not dwell much on this for she had problems to face.

She conferred with Abner and it was agreed that he was to have a home with them as long as he should live in exchange for his labor. As for the boy she felt there was no alternative but to keep him and treat him as one of the family. This attitude reflected to her credit, for she was under no obligation to him except that imposed by her humanity. She was not aware that Danny was her husband's son; only one person knew this and a vow made when the mare ran before the threat of his blow sealed his lips. She loved Danny but not as her own son, and many another under the circumstances would have sent him alone into the world without pity for his homelessness.

When she had decided that he should stay she called him to her and told him that his home was with them if he so desired it, and because of the look on his face when she had told him she was glad she did.

So, making such a settlement of her affairs, she knew a gray peace, and because of this peace she could sleep in the night.

7

DANNY

Danny lay in his bed. The last light of the sun was fading from the tops of the hills he could see through the north window. He was so recently wakened he was uncertain whether the country beyond the window was actual or an extension of the landscape of sleep from whence he was newly arrived in the world of waking. He had been wakened by fear. In the country of sleep he came face to face with the dead Preacher. The ruined face of the dead Preacher confronted him and the mouth opened to speak, and its word was a blob of blood. He woke immediately and looked toward the bed nearest the window, the best bed, where his uncle slept, but his uncle was not there.

Because it was yet light it was too early for his uncle to be in his bed. He heard the others below stairs, recognizing each by a particular sound, and he followed them in his mind as they went about. The old woman Mercidy was by the stove washing the dishes. He heard the clay sound of plates against each other and the tin sounds of knives and forks rattling in the pan. The kitchen door slammed and he saw in his mind the great Abner with a pail of slop leaving the kitchen, his ponderous step taking him in a slow waddle in the direction of the pigpen. Mary crooned to Joshua who gurgled in pleasure, or sent forth now and then peevish cries that rang dissonantly in the evening air. He heard, not the sound but the silence of Jason, and he saw him sitting contained in a corner of the kitchen, the quiet, watchful stare of his eyes steadfast before him. A cord of expectancy tightened within him when he thought of Jason, and for a moment he was not surprised that no sound below identified his uncle.

He lay in his bed because they said he was sick. He was not sick. He flexed his muscles and felt the customary strength of his body building to tensions under his skin. The strength that propelled him through the full and active day before he was sick was renewed in his body, but he would remain in his bed until another sun's rising because it would please the others. It would please the old woman Mercidy, and through the sounds of those below stairs that came to him muffled and faint like sounds heard under water he was remembering the words of the old woman:

"Tomorrow you can get up. Lie still until tomorrow."

So he lay in his bed and the sun was far over in the sky of today. It was not long till he could get up again. Tomorrow was a yard of sun and the width of night away.

He was glad to please the old woman Mercidy. When the gray wolf of death had yowled at him in hunger the old woman gave the wolf her hand to gnaw. Then, when he was sick, he was not afraid of the wolf even but now that he felt his strength flow back from its dispersal into the emptiness left by his uncle's going the thought of the wolf of death frightened him. He was glad the old woman fooled the wolf by offering him her bony hand.

Tomorrow, he thought.

Tomorrow the sun on the frosty world and the sight of their faces bearing witness that he was not alone. The face of Mercidy, of Mary, of Abner; the face of the Idiot Ezra with the peace of sleep upon every feature.

The face of Jason.

With something of shock then it occurred to him that there were two faces he could not recall. He did not remember the face of the infant Joshua. And the face of his uncle was from him forever. When he tried to think of the face of his Uncle Enid his head went dark like a room where a candle is extinguished. The image of his uncle's face was usurped in his mind by darkness edged about with a whirring sound as of the departing wings of many doves.

8

U N C L E   E N I D

On the night after the Preacher's funeral, which he attended because not to have done so would have pointed a finger of suspicion at his relationship with Mary, Uncle Enid lay in his bed until he was certain the whole household was asleep. The events of the last few days moved in erratic pageantry through his mind as they had moved through reality, grim, morose, almost insupportable in their unrelieved portentousness. The fear he had known when the mare ran under the threat of his blow remained in his mind, and his whole being was keyed to tension awaiting one event: To escape.

The world was wide, and now he felt impelled anew by the current of movement that had been set in motion when he sold the farm. The impetus of his need to escape this place added to the power of that current as a stream's flow is strengthened by flood, and he was astonished, now that he thought about it, that that flow could ever have been dammed behind so flimsy a barrier as his physical love for a married woman, for Mary.

He was not easy in his mind about Mary. Now that the barrier to their love had fallen in the death of the Preacher he saw that he had been grateful for the barrier and had not really wished it removed. Yet he hesitated in his contemplated action of going away because somewhere in his being a tribunal sat that convicted him of betrayal, until he remembered the look she had given him at the funeral. She clearly repudiated him then with her eyes. At the time he was surprised and somewhat hurt but now his spirit knew a lift because of the repudiation and he did not pursue the reason, was only grateful for it because it set him free.

He had not meant to sleep this night, yet he slept and when he was asleep he was in the weather of the first dream he had had on the night of the Preacher's wake. He was climbing in the gray void, and he climbed nimbly because he had lost the weights from his feet. Just before he reached the top of the cliff on which he climbed his sleeping mind recognized the dream and he woke.

At first he was frantic, thinking he might have slept too long. He needed enough of darkness to blanket his going beyond the borders of that county. When he looked at his watch he saw that it was a little beyond the midnight hour.

He dressed in his best clothes, those he had worn to the funeral. Then he sat a moment on his bed looking into the dark toward the back of the attic where Danny lay. The lament for Danny began again in his heart. The tears fell in his heart, and as he made his way to the stairs, stealthily to avoid waking any of the household, his feet of their own volition carried him to Danny's bed. He stood a moment curbing his breathing, then his hand explored the darkness and found Danny's face. He removed his hand quickly lest it wake him. He stooped slowly forward and touched Danny's forehead with his lips.

Danny's breathing came warm into his neck and he experienced such a wrench in his spirit he almost cried aloud. He was on the verge of lifting Danny in his arms and carrying him with him into the night, into the uncertainty of his own future, and then he had a vision of him secure in the family of his father. He saw him established with his brothers in that household and in time inheriting his portion of his father's estate. The taint of the Preacher was for a moment on Danny's flesh, but in loyalty to their former togetherness

and to the blood of his sister he put thoughts of it from him
and carried forth with him a love for Danny that was whole
and pure as long as he lived.

When Danny stirred in his sleep he turned quickly from
him and descended the stairs. When he stepped forth from
the house onto the road his heart was as dark as the night that
closed around him. But once on his way he began to think
of the whole of the dream he had on the night of the Preacher's wake, and thinking in terms of the dream he felt his feet
grow light, losing their weights; and after a while, far to the
east, he saw the gestating light of the sun that would break
at length like the great illumination he beheld when in the
dream he looked over the cliff's top and was a new man.

On the road he thought suddenly of the lost coin again.
He turned it about with the fingers of his mind, and the
thought struck him that he was still asleep and dreaming for
one side of the coin bore the image of Danny and when he
turned it over he saw that the head on the obverse side was
Jason's.

One foot after the other, he thought, one foot after the
other. It became a refrain that kept time with his steps that
carried him farther and farther from that household, though
the wide world of his thoughts and dreams approached so
slowly he seemed to himself to be treading a treadmill.

The next morning they woke to find him gone, and they
never heard of him again.

9

DANNY

When he learned that his uncle had gone without word of return he went all that day in a stupor. The next morning he went to his uncle's bed and when he found it empty still he stood by the head of the bed a moment and then began to cry. Long racking sobs shook him while he clung to the bed-post. After a while he collapsed and lay on the floor while the Idiot stared at him from the edge of his own bed.

He sobbed all day, complaining of darkness when the others asked what hurt him. At first they thought he had suddenly gone blind, but when they held their hands before his eyes and said, "See it?" he answered "Yes" impatiently while he shook his head from side to side. He tried to break from them and go hide but when he had gone a few steps the strength flowed out of his legs and he sagged to the floor.

Finally Mary sent the great Abner riding for the doctor, who came and examined him and sat staring at him with round empty eyes, pulling at his lower lip with finger and thumb.

"What ails the boy?" Mary asked. But her voice spoke only of her own loss and grief, and he suddenly saw the dead Preacher, shrouded in his shroud, lying white and motionless in Mary's words.

"Nothing," the doctor said.

"Nothing!" Mary echoed incredulously, and the Preacher vanished from her voice and Danny saw his own face mirrored there, but when he heard the doctor's words he was afraid for it was not natural to be sick without ailment. He lay in his semistupor; the doctor's round eyes were upon him and he wished vainly for the strength that had flowed after his uncle so that he might escape them and lie somewhere in dark peace.

"Nothing is physically wrong with the boy," the doctor said when he continued. "I'd say he had suffered a severe emotional shock."

He heard the words as if from a great distance, almost without interest, as if they did not apply to himself.

"His uncle," Mary said, and her voice was threaded with bitterness, "he walked off and left him. He was the only relative he had." And she gave the circumstances of his uncle's coming and going from that household.

The doctor nodded his head up and down, his round eyes fixed on Danny's face so that they rolled like counter-weighted marbles with his nodding.

"Yes," he said after a while, "that would do it."

"Why does he say he can't see?" Mary asked, for to her that was a greater mystery than the fact of his illness.

"He sees outside what is inside himself, only darkness. Because his only emotional tie has been broken neither the past nor the future exists for him. His past was tied to his uncle and when he went from the boy he took his past with him, the future does not exist because he doesn't want it to exist without his uncle. Direction has been taken suddenly from his life."

As the doctor spoke the darkness edged with wings was in his mind, and for the first time he accepted the fact of his loss. His uncle would not return. Or even if he should return the cleavage between them was now absolute; it was validated by his illness itself. He knew now why he was sick, and at the moment he understood why he was sick he saw that at length he would be well again and go whole and complete into the full and active day.

"Any life that lacks direction is blind," the doctor said,

keeping his round eyes on Danny. He took his pipe from his pocket and held it in his hand without lighting it.

"What can we do?" Mary said.

"Do you love him?" the doctor said.

"Yes," Mary said, "we love him." But again the dead Preacher haunted her words.

"Then find his uncle," the doctor said, "or replace him in the boy's affections." And that was his only prescription.

Mercidy came into the room and told Mary the child cried in her bedroom. Mary went to the child and the old woman waited courteously on the doctor.

"I hate suffering," the doctor said rising to go. "Suffering, suffering," he said in a tired mumble to himself.

"In a narrow country we suffer no more," the old woman said, "but we prefer the wide one of pain."

The doctor widened his round empty eyes at the old woman as he went from the room.

Abner went into the country, riding for two days, but no one had seen his uncle, or had news of him.

For the first few days after his uncle vanished he slept below stairs, in the old women's bed, and when he wakened in the night and thoughts of his uncle sent him into sobs the patient old voice spoke to him, chittering at times like a bird to its young, and when he looked to verify her presence he saw Mercidy sitting in her rocking chair, a quilt about her shoulders. Her hands lay idle in her lap and they were gnarled and ruined; it was as if she held in her lap two eagle's claws filched from some hunter's trophies.

She waited upon him night and day, as if she feared to relax her vigil for a moment lest death take him while her back was turned. The others, no matter how they loved him, complained to the old woman that she was overtaxing her strength. But she only rocked impatiently in her chair and told them to mind their own business.

"If death is hungry let him have a bone to gnaw," she said. When he heard this he looked at the joined bones that lay at peace in her lap.

On a night during her vigil he woke from sleep and looking toward her chair he saw her shrouded in white. She sat shrouded in white by the low-turned lamp, and an animal-like sound of fear came shaking from his lips and she stirred from her immobile pose, her head emerged from the shroud and she was the old woman his grandmother who had lain on the boards between two chairs eight years before. When he was fully wakened he saw that the face was Mercidy's and yet the transformation had been accomplished, and the loss of his uncle was lessened by one.

One day after he began to mend and was allowed to be up an hour or so each day Abner came from the barn with news. Flora, the spotted cow, had freshened in the night. When he opened her door to pass through her feed that morning he saw that a bull calf, wet yet from his mother's laundering tongue, pulled with energy at her swollen teats.

Abner conferred with Mary in undertones and then came to Danny and said to come with him to the barn.

In Flora's stall the bull calf tugged at its mother still. When they opened the door he turned his head to look at them and wrinkled his nose in the manner of young calves and gamboled once in the littered stall.

"He is yours," Abner said. "What will you call him?"

"I'll call him Abner," he said to show his gratitude for the gift. He stood filled with joy at the ownership of the calf.

Abner's huge hand was a great weight on his shoulder, and when he turned after a while and waddled in the direction of the house he left off looking at the calf and came by Abner's side.

"How would it be if *I* was your uncle?" Abner said.

"You can be my uncle," he said. "You can be my Uncle Abner." And strangely at that moment the great Abner's bulk diminished, melted and flowed away into thin air, and his Uncle Enid looked from the eyes of Abner. Later he was Abner again but the metamorphosis was not invalidated, and the loss of his uncle was less by two.

At length he said to himself, my mother Mary, my grandmother Mercidy, my uncle Abner, my brother Ezra, my brother Joshua. Then he paused in his recital, remembering how the bars had fallen from Jason's eyes:

On the seventh day of his illness he was restored to his own bed and the Idiot, who slept now with his mother, was in his bed no more. Withdrawn from the presence of the old woman Mercidy, he felt again the emptiness he had experienced when he discovered the flight of his uncle, and he lay disconsolate in his bed while the sun failed and the others gathered for the evening meal below stairs.

Later he heard the sound of Jason's foot upon the stair, and he knew again the feeling of expectancy that tightened in his breast at the other's approach. Darkness was in the attic with a depth like the sea's. He heard the step of Jason wading in this darkness, and his feet did not pause at the middle bed where he had always slept but continued to his own. He had not even time for conjecture before he heard the sound of Jason's clothes dropping to the floor. He lay still and silent, his head turned from where Jason stood naked, though it was completely dark, for he guarded in his mind the inviolateness of Jason's flesh.

In a moment Jason turned the covers from him and lay down by his side. Without a word indicating how his spirit strove to burst its shell of loneliness and find its brother, Jason placed his arm across his chest. And at his touch the inveterate angels of love and death leaned together in agreement and donned their third immortal face, which is life's, and he slept in the chaste embrace of his brother Jason.

The next day when they were in each other's presence, and in the sun's, he saw that the bars had fallen from Jason's eyes and they were never erected again.

Though the weather of grief was upon that house, life there went forward as usual. The activities of the farm were resumed shortly after the Preacher's funeral and were interrupted only by Abner's search for Danny's uncle. On his return without news, Abner and Jason began to gather in the harvest against the winter. They rode in the wagon heaped and groaning beneath the mounded corn and Abner waved his great arms and shouted at the mules that strained on their toes before the reluctant wheels.

Because Mercidy would not allow him to go to the fields with Jason and Abner, Danny did the chores of the barnyard and fed the pigs with pails of slop from the kitchen. The hens followed him about, speaking so companionably in their chirring tongue they won him from indifference to their kind. The bull calf Abner gave him ran races with its shadow in the barn lot and shied at imaginary dangers in the full light of day. Danny felt the bonds that held him to this place strengthened as he went among the barnyard creatures.

In the house the women carried on their work as usual, though now because of Joshua more and more of it fell to the lot of the old woman Mercidy. She cooked and washed and ironed, and then, as if these activities were not enough, in moments that were otherwise idle she sat knitting in her chair, resting and nodding in sleep at intervals.

So the days passed.

Each day when there was no more light Abner and Jason came to the house and sat down to supper silent from exhaustion. Jason's face was pinched and drawn from incessant labor, and after stooping for the corn all day he rose from sitting bent down like an old man. But because of the elasticity of his youth his body soon put off stiffness, and when he moved about there was a new confidence in his bearing. Danny ate by Jason's side as he had done before, but now Jason's hands were not upon him like the beaks of birds in teasing playfulness. They sat side by side without touch or word passing between them, and if Jason looked at him there was no longer challenge in his still, shut stare. When Jason looked at him now it was without craft or promise or taunt. It was with the gaze of one who looks into a mirror and sees reflected there a true image of himself.

Each time as soon as he had eaten Abner rose and yawned, stretching his arms outward from the shoulders as if he were crucified upon the tree of sleep. Then with a benevolent face he ambled from them in the direction of his lean-to and soon they would hear the sounds of his snores shaking at the timbers of the room.

After supper Mercidy would sit knitting determinedly in her chair by the fire, her attitude a flag of defiance in the face of circumstance. She felt deeply the loss of her only son who had made her proud because he stood before the people, yet because yielding to her loss by senseless grief or lassitude would not restore him she refused to bow down to these. At times she sang snatches of songs that rose in her memory, and she sang because she enjoyed it and not to make a great noise in the ear of emptiness. When Mary chided the old woman and said she was exhausting her strength she answered,

"I will be still in the grave. I will long to stretch my old bones in their long confinement, but I may not. I will stretch them now."

Mary tended the infant Joshua, looking at him at times as if surprised by his presence in her lap. At other times she hugged him to her suddenly and fiercely as if he were such a treasure men build vaults to protect.

"Boodle, boodle, boodle!" Ezra cried on all occasions, and

the pure peace, as of sleep, that was upon his countenance communciated itself mysteriously to the others; and the great stone of their grief began to wear away and lessen in the stream of ordinary affairs.

In the depth of night they slept, and in the morning, when the watchful fowls from promontories on every hand descried in the east the resurrection of light, wakened.

THE END